DEATH METAL EPIC
I: The Inverted Katabasis

ATLATL

Dean Swinford

Atlatl Press
POB 292644
Dayton, Ohio 45429

Death Metal Epic (Book One: The Inverted Katabasis)
Copyright © 2013 by Dean Swinford
ISBN-13: 978-0-9883484-3-1
ISBN-10: 0988348438

Cover art and design copyright © 2013 by Matthew Revert
www.matthewrevert.com

The Inverted Katabasis

The First Book
of the
Death Metal Epic

Table of Contents

Table of Contents

Part 2

Part One

Such as among them were convict of great and heinous trespasses, them they condemned into stone-quarries, and into mines to dig metal, there to be kept in chains all the days of their life.
   —Thomas More, *Utopia*

I don't mean to dwell
But I can't help myself
When I feel the vibe
And taste a memory
Of a time in life
When years seemed to stand still.
   —Death, "Symbolic"

1. Metametal: The Intro

How do you start a death metal epic?

In epic form, of course. You have to invoke the muse. Not Calliope, the beautiful voiced, but the very form of the voice of dread. A different muse. Its voice suggests its form. Its voices suggest its forms. In one guise, gaunt. Sepulchral. She is an ageless cadaver strapped in burning leather. In another, an octopoid—or is it serpentine—malevolence creeping along the ocean floor. At times it takes the form of a living dead book fashioned from human flesh.

All of these.

None of these.

A perverse trinity perverting the Trinity.

What kind of invocation does it demand?

First, you'd have to think of it like a death metal album itself. And you know they all start with Intros and end with Outros. It doesn't matter that Outro's not a word in any other context. Here, it works perfectly. You can use the same keyboard or the same special effects CD that you used for the Intro, but with a different ominous vocal track. Or you can just repeat the Intro to enhance the ritualistic feeling of circularity.

So for this one, a death metal epic, a devastating avalanche of genres, including the Künstlerroman and the *Tombeau*, we'd have to begin in a manner true to form, with a death metal intro:

Sounds (layered via 4-track):

Chains dragged across an unfinished basement floor.

Some kind of infernal Thomas train engine chuffing at 45 rpm, then played and recorded at 33 rpm.

Tormented screams of the dudes draining the 24-pack in the studio.

Vokill:

On top of all of this, a slurupy grunting, a voice evoking the body of an ogre, orc, overfed Northern European postadolescent, or the stern authoritarian voice spurring the demented impulses plaguing the mentally ill:

Prepare to enter an infernal realm of utter debastation

(with the echo on the last word, so we hear: "station –ation – ation fading into the dragged chain slow train abyss. And annunciated so everyone can hear the gothic font you used to print out your lyrics)

You stand at the gate of fractured dreams

(here the chorus of tortured acquaintances really meshes with the chain track as your audience enters the dungeon of impure dominions)

And then you're at the kicker. You're getting down to the title, that phrase that names your work, that phrase you'll be shouting at the sky, the ceiling of some rickety club, the glaring eye of a suspended klieg light, for at least the next year or so, if you're lucky and (more importantly) really put your back into it right here, right now, on this very bellow:

Death Metal Epic

You want to pause a moment for effect. Let the echo carry the words into the deepest headphone recesses:

𝔦𝔱 . . . 𝔦𝔱 . . . 𝔦𝔱

But you don't want them to think you're dumb, do you? Sure, most of the people are just going to see it and write you off: Death metal? Oh great, they'll say. Epic? Epically lame is more like it. Just what the world needs. Another brainless flogging, they'll say, all kill kill kill and death death death. Most of them won't see past that. They'll go off and buy those Bowie reissues instead. Even worse are the ones who want all kill kill kill, who flip through the stacks muttering death death death to themselves in a mindless trance.

You know, your fanbase.

But there's more to it, death metal, isn't there? You want them both—fans and nonfans alike—to think, arise, elevate themselves by sinking into the abyss. An ascent through descent. You want to give them a clue, a hint of the eternal legacy they've tapped into, the way downtuned guitars resuscitate long dead gods—

Baphomet

Cernunnos

Dionysus

The chaos gods. The inbetweeners. Both good and evil. The ones we've forgotten. Not dead, but dreaming.

You take a sip of milk, whole exclusively, to really coat those vocal cords, then spit it out, your subtitle, the clue, the second line of the chorus:

𝔗𝔥𝔢 𝔍𝔫𝔳𝔢𝔯𝔱𝔢𝔡 𝔎𝔞𝔱𝔞𝔟𝔞𝔰𝔦𝔰

The mythical journey to hell. Inverted. Like a crucifix. A journey from hell? No answer. Just silence. Divine knowledge encased in its blackness. A brief moment of silence for the fallen—

Euronymous

Chuck Schuldiner

Quorthon

2. Minimum Wage

Why do I listen to heavy metal? It's a question I get a lot. "What do you get out of it?" my co-workers ask me. "Heavy metal has no soul," they say. No feeling. It's too loud. Too guitar frenzied. And the lyrics? All this stuff about Satan and violence adds nothing to human culture. An excursion into the world of heavy metal is a strictly adolescent affair best completed before you get your driver's license. File away the Ozzy records and get on with your life.

I am not getting on with my life, musically or otherwise.

And for me, Ozzy counts as easy listening. What I really like, what I love, sounds like a Gremlin in a blender. I love the wayward paths and forgotten chasms of metal's chthonic kingdom. Death metal, with its monstrous croaks and rhythmic, spasm-inducing riffs. Black metal's eerie hymns to long-dead Nordic gods. A sullen, despondent, doom metal dirge. These, and the endless products of inter-generic cross pollinations, grind core, death thrash, dark ambient, resound in ways that the pop music I'm supposed to like—the Beatles, Michael Jackson, any musician currently marketing perfume or energy drinks—does not.

I can't get on with my life. I'm always looking for some new release that will make me feel how I felt the first time I heard Queen's "We Will Rock You" (age 6), Mötley Crüe's "Shout at the Devil" (age 10), or Morbid Angel's "Chapel of Ghouls" (age 15). I want to relive that first shiver of power.

Feel sounds that give, and threaten with, power. Worship those sounds, that power. Any true metal fan wants the same thing. It's a complex paradox. The object of a perennial quest.

What am I looking for? You could call it a goat song. Another guy, a bandmate, explained that one to me. We'll get to it.

I'm not just a fan. I'm a guitarist, too. I want to create the goat song. They call me Azrael. It's a stage name, like "Prince" or "MC Hammer," if those guys hit the stage in a whirlwind of hair, spikes, and corpsepaint. Angel of death. Or help of god. Not really a stage name. It's a metal name, like Trey Azagthoth, Legion, or Xytraguptor. There is a difference. It's changed from album to album. Or at least mine did. On *Infernö* (the umlaut is nö typö), I was Azrael le Fevers.

The name started as a joke, evolved over time. It's in the liner notes of the first Valhalla album, *Thrones of Satanic Dominion*. That's the death metal band I joined in high school. The label guys, Sean and Mike at Plutonic Records, couldn't just put "guitar." Instead, they put our initials, then these kind of over the top descriptions for each of us. Call it a marketing ploy. Mine said "D.: Angel of Six String Death." That's why all the artsy indie rockers and angry punks I work with constantly mock metal. They think the hyperbole is always serious.

Before all that, I was just "David." I still am. It says so on my nametag. I work fulltime at a bookstore. A few weeks ago, right after Thanksgiving and at the start of the retail rush, a couple of the guys I work with found the label maker lying on the table in the breakroom. They crack on my metalness, page "Lord Azrael to register" over the store intercom. The managers hate that.

We personalized our nametags—"Steveorama," "Dan the Man," we even played with my metal name a bit and printed out a new one, "Azraelington Maximus." It barely fit, the taped fringe "mus" fluttering off the edge. Azraelington Maxi—for maximum absorbency.

You'd think mine might have generated the customer

complaint that led to the managerial nametag crackdown, but it was actually "Steveorama." According to Lisa, our manager, we needed accurate nametags so the customers could lodge accurate complaints. On Christmas day, "Steveorama" said to another worker that he'd wished the swarms of book browsers were at home, visiting family, going to church even, anything other than shopping mindlessly on the holiday. He almost lost his job. People are so sensitive this time of year.

You may know Valhalla. *Thrones of Satanic Dominion* sold just under 2,000 copies. That's huge in the metal underground. If you're really a fan, a tape collector or someone who reads smudgy Xeroxed zines like *Cerebral Holocaust* or *Democide*, you might have even listened to or read about our first release, the *Zombichrist* EP. Limited edition tape. Hand numbered to 666 copies.

Probably not. I still have 237 cassettes crammed into my closet.

I'm just the guy working the help desk at the Booksalot superstore. And it's looking like this is the only stage I'll be playing in the near future. I'm twenty-one. I am not in college. I'm not even taking night classes at the community college or enrolled in a correspondence program leading to a rewarding career as a medical records file clerk or auto body welder. I am, in other words, a loser. And the only things I had—that tape, that CD—are disappearing into the past. The rest of my band—Phil, John, even Jake—have moved on, left Miami for the college life in Tallahassee. When we stood on stage at The Masquerade in Tampa, our blastbeats pummeling a "star studded" audience filled with dudes from bands like Morbid Angel, Monstrosity, and Death, I never thought it would end like this. When we finished our set at the Button South, all of Bolt Thrower (over from England and at the start of their *Warmaster* US tour) watching us, I did not worry about the SAT scheduled early the next morning.

If you came in on one of those dead days between Christmas and New Year's, at a time when the early nineties started to ripen and mature into the mid-nineties, maybe looking for something to help you with your past, *Toxic Parents*, say, or a mystical plan for your future, something initiated by Carlos Castaneda in one of his infinite incarnations, maybe just looking for some post-Christmas sale items, you'd see me at the help desk next to Lisa, the manager, and Claire, the corduroy-overalled punk rocker who, despite her multiple piercings and saffron shock of dyed hair, should really run the place.

I'd be the tallish guy with longish hair. Tall enough so they page me to haul books down from the top shelves, but not tall enough to stuff a ball through a hoop. The good thing about working for this media megastore and not its more profitable competitor is they like their going nowhere employees to look kind of "edgy." We're going nowhere in style. I think the managers picked us to fill some series of subculture profiles compiled by the central office and distributed to each store. We've got the punk rocker, the skate rat, a smattering of club kids, a person of indeterminate gender, some bleached Victorian types, and me, the resident Hessian, a real bargain at $5.15 an hour.

On most days, I'm wearing this or that heavy metal shirt. There are limits to edginess, though, some guidelines I've intuited through my year here.

An occult symbol or two is okay—not too many customers familiar with the Nekronomikon's endless iconography—but an inverted cross is a no-no. Unless you can't really notice it because it's in the midst of an indecipherable icicle font, like on my Unleashed shirt.

Medieval themes are okay, even the battle scenes of impaled Cornish knights bristling like pincushions on my Amorphis shirt.

The main rule seems to be no "modern" gore or violence. Nothing that could happen in a newspaper. My Cannibal Corpse shirt, for example, has never been poked by a nametag.

Medical tools and incomprehensible definitions for painful

medical procedures, on the other hand, are a go. My Carcass *Necroticism* shirt has generated zero customer complaints.

Those are the managerial rules, but you've got to watch out for your coworkers, too. Anything too gothy will lead to a day of endless mockery by the punk and indie types. On the day I'd worn my Moonspell shirt (pointy symmetrical logo? Check. Pentagram? Check. Mystical image of an ibex horned moon goddess? Check. Pseudo-occult ESL lyrics? Double-check), Claire followed me around all day, saying "David, that is absolutely *retarded*!" and chanting the lyrics quoted on my back:

"'Queen in silk, skin like milk,'" another line or two of poetries, then the singer's metal name, "Langsuyar."

By the end of the day, I'd become Langsuyar:

"Langsuyar to the help desk."

"Langsuyar, page 222."

"Langsuyar to the cafe."

• • •

I checked my watch. I'd told John (J.: Subterranean Tremors), our bassist, to come by at noon for my lunch break. He and his brother Phil (P.: Imperial Devastation by Phrygian Tones) [i.e.—lead guitar] had driven down from college for winter break.

Jake's down, too. You know, "J: Wardrums." I was surprised when he moved. In keeping with the age-old stereotype of the idiot drummer, he's up there with them, but isn't enrolled yet. He's there in body, if not in mind, taking his prerecs at Tallahassee Community College. But who am I to call anyone an idiot? Jake and John moved up in August, right after finishing high school. I graduated three years ago.

Phil went first, last year. We weren't sure how it would work having our lead guitarist at the other end of the peninsula, but he'd trekked the turnpike like a trooper, pulling up in his weather beaten Honda just as we unloaded our gear at this or that gig.

That's the year our album came out, too. You could find it at any music store. If you special ordered it. Then waited a week or two. Maybe three. I filled out my application here— Have you ever been arrested? If yes, why? Do you agree to submit to random drug screening? If no, why not?—around the same time John and Jake took their SATs. After I deposited that first royalty check, I worked my way through some more personalized word problems involving rent and ramen noodles. Death metal, you may be surprised to learn, offers no easy path to fortune. I quickly realized the band's true earning potential. The number of dollars deposited might have covered an electric bill or two.

Even though it was almost New Year's, and the rest of the guys had been in town for over a week, I'd barely seen them. I stared at the front door waiting for John to come in so I could take a break and clock out.

When he did, any excitement I felt faded as soon as I saw him. He pushed through the doors looking like a shining beacon in crimson and gold. He wore a Seminole sweatshirt and khakis with sharp, crisp pleats. He took off his Seminole baseball hat to reveal a shaggy side part, barely covering his ears. The long mop he'd spin while playing was gone. He'd been sheared.

I nervously fingered the edges of my still-long hair and had one thought: the band faced certain doom.

We sat on the tiled patio at the front of the store, me munching Pop Tarts and swilling a cup of coffee from the cafe (one of the few job perks I enjoyed, free coffee, kept me in a perpetual caffeinated jitter—at night, my teeth gnashed like frenetic blastbeats) and John smoking a cigarette. At least he still smokes, I thought, until I smelled the burnt cinnamon smoke of a clove. That's what hippies smoke between bong rips.

The band faced its own imperial devastation.

Appearances can be deceiving, though. Perhaps there's hope. Phil had, after all, lived there for a year with no ill effects. And Jake, who'd worn a spiked dog collar in his senior yearbook picture? He was better equipped to resist this bucolic realm of easy living. But as we talked, I realized this was it. They'd gone soft. Now that they were all together up there, far from the seething maelstrom of south Florida, scrotal heat rashes and endless traffic, death metal meant nothing to them. It was just the perverse soundtrack of high-school nostalgia.

John put his arm on my shoulder and looked in my eyes like he was breaking up, sweetly, with his high school sweetheart.

"Those times were cool and all, but that's not all there is out there. Plus, the money sucked. I think I used what I made to buy a microwave oven."

He made it seem like he still cared.

"David, you could play with us, too. You know that Jake moved up. We're getting a place off campus next semester. Phil's already moved out of the dorms."

I tried to appeal to his emotions, that thrill we felt in middle school as we made mixtapes from our meager collections. Metallica, Slayer, Testament on his. DRI, Suicidal, King Diamond on mine.

"Come on, John," I whined. "What about..." and here I made the sign of the horns, index and pinky raised, "EVIL? What about rock?"

But then he went too far.

"You know that's all bullshit. Besides, it's not like we stopped playing music together. We're in a band. A new one. Smokey the Band."

I stared into my coffee, crestfallen. Weed humor.

"Besides, there're actually girls at our gigs now."

Our band had been undone by dormitories and intercollegiate athletics. I almost left right then.

Instead, I tried one final gambit. I brought up The Contract. It's what kept me going. Out of fear or hope, I couldn't tell. We'd signed a two album deal. The next album would have to be bigger, right? And from there, maybe we'd move to a bigger record label. Besides, the contract called for a tour, a chance to get away from *The Celestine Prophecies* and John Grisham. We were supposed to tour over the summer.

In Europe.

Where people actually like heavy metal.

I fantasized about the contract, another album, a European tour, every day. Above all, it promised a chance to get away from Lisa who, just then, poked her head out the front door, her glaring eyes framed by platinum Darth Vader bangs.

"David, you know you can't sit out here."

Management had waged a campaign against more than personalized nametags. They also didn't want us to sit in front of the store on our breaks. Instead, they'd generously provided a break table. Out back. By the dumpster. Within earshot of a Burger King drive thru.

She mouthed the next part.

"The customers might see you."

"Sorry," I mumbled.

She looked at her watch, turned, and went inside.

I stood up and checked the time. For whom the bell tolls.

"Look, I'll call you later, John."

As I walked past the business books, past *Who Touched My Cheese?* and *What Color is Your Parachute?*, I fought the urge to scream.

What color is my parachute?

Black.

Polka dotted with pentagrams.

An infernal dirigible
plunging
down
down
down.

At some point, I would no longer be a musician who worked at a bookstore. I would just be the guy at the bookstore who used to be a musician.

3. Juan Bon Joker

"You realize that Valhalla is still under contract, right?"

I pressed the phone to my ear and covered my head with my hand as I hunched over the help desk. After John left, all I could think about was the contract. I asked Claire for advice. She said I should call the label and try to get out of it. I didn't really want to get out of it, because then what would I have? What would I think about during the endless hours of pulling each and every book to the exact edge of the shelf? How else would I stave off the pernicious sounds of Paul Simon's *Graceland*, which streamed from the store speakers on infinite repeat? But she had a point. You can't make an album and go on tour with a band that no longer exists. A dead metal band.

"Use your words, Langsuyar," she'd said, flipping through *Maximum Rock and Roll.* "And don't let Lisa see you."

I tried.

"Yeah, I totally realize that, Sean, it's just that I'm basically the lone Viking left manning the Valhalla ship."

"David, we need an album. Soon. Besides, a new one will help sell the old one."

"It's not like I can make an album by myself."

He continued like he hadn't heard me.

"And you still have your touring obligation. We put out one record and so we've got to get you guys going on a tour and a second one. At the very least you need to tour this summer, get your name out there. You don't even need the whole band for that. Otherwise, all of you are in violation of the contract, a legally binding contract."

I thought of John romancing some poli-sci major by the Sof-Serv ice cream machine in the university cafetorium, chatting her up after handing her a flyer for the next Smokey the Band jamfest. And me, every day, toiling away in this place. Clock in. Shelve books. Man the register. My every action accompanied by the endless loop of Paul Simon's voice, one world beat Möbius strip of sound. I tapped a paper clip against the desk.

"Uh . . . excuse me . . . can you help me find a book?"

A customer. And a jingling sound, like the help bell that only true assholes ever rang. It wasn't loud enough to be the bell, though. It sounded like some distant reindeer herd.

Was it Santa Claus from the mall?

I sighed. Why can't people just browse?

"Sean, I promise I'll talk to the guys. I've got to go."

"Remember: legally binding."

I hung up. The jingling bells still reverberated across the help desk. How was that going to work? Who ever heard of a one man metal band, live and on tour?

"Can I help you?" I hissed, my paper clip now a mangled mess.

The stress was getting to me. I needed to cut down on coffee, free or not. A Renaissance fair refugee stood in front of me. It wasn't Santa from the mall, but it could have been one of his elves. This guy, short and Latino, wore a billowy frilly smock of the kind last sported by Shelley. He'd topped the smock with a brown leather vest fringed with tiny bells. He was dressed to board frigates.

A taffeta headscarf, cut from a flag, or maybe a blood red prom dress, contained a shock of wild black hair. He'd cinched the scarf, Rambo style, right above his thick black eyebrows. A plaited ponytail hung halfway down his back.

"I'm looking for a book." He was courteous, his voice more cultivated than the average Miamian. He sounded as suave as

George Hamilton looks.

"It's called *The White Goddess*. It's by Robert Graves."

"Graves ... Graves. ..." I typed the name into the computer. I could feel his hard stare at my chest. I had on an old Candlemass shirt, the one for *Ancient Dreams*. I got it when John and I first started playing music together. He and Phil had it on gatefold vinyl, put a couple songs on those early mix tapes, and I thought the cover, an edenic garden scene, sky blue and gold, taken from some 19th century painting, looked so classy in contrast to the therapy art used for so many other album covers.

Something the parents would approve of, I'd thought at the time. Something to show them the piano and guitar lessons had been worth it. They'd almost canceled them when I sat at the dinner table in the first metal shirt I'd bought, a Slayer shirt with a throned goat presiding over a trio of bishops bobbing in boiled blood.

"I like your shirt."

"Thanks," I said absently, scanning the computer screen. "Graves ... here it is. Mythology. Follow me."

I stepped around the desk. His costume was comprehensive. He wore fringed knee high moccasins. As we walked across the store, he swished and jangled like a belled cat. He even had a brass bell hanging from one ear. He had a tiny acoustic guitar, ukulele-sized, but with a compact, nearly triangular body, strapped to his back. I'd never seen a guitar quite like it; I wondered how it played.

"Are you into Lore?"

The way he said it, I thought he meant a band. "Lore." It sounded doomy, like Candlemass. Something forlorn and direful.

He didn't let me answer.

"You seem like you might be. Not many people are, these days."

"Lore?"

"You know, the imaginary, the stories and images that never really die, but keep repeating, even here in this ridiculous city. That's a Thomas Cole painting on your shirt. 'The Course of Empire.' He would have loved painting this place, shown it swallowed by the sea."

If you're not from Miami, you'd be surprised how many locals hate the place. And not just the ones, like me, indentured to its service economy. We stopped at the mythology section, a shoulder-high half shelf topped with a plastic ivy in a "Greek urn" next to a squat stone gargoyle, the bestial offspring of a bowling ball and a garden gnome.

I scanned the shelf, found the book, and handed it to him. It wasn't hard to find. The spine was bright yellow with black writing, like a traffic sign.

"I've been looking for this for awhile. I thought I'd have to special order it." He started flipping through the pages.

"What's it for?" He'd sparked my curiosity. The book was thick. It looked serious. Unlike most of the books people actually bought, it had no pictures, except for a sketch of some weird symbols, three ladies, a snake, a pentagram, on the cover.

"I'm doing a bit of reading for a tattoo I'm getting. It's going to be of the Ouroboros, here, around my heart."

"The Ouroboros?" I had no clue. It sounded like the name of a sandwich. An Ouroboros deluxe, extra pickles.

"You've never heard of it?"

"No. What is it?"

"A mythical creature. No—more importantly—it is *the* mythical creature, the creature at the center of every story, a creature that lies at the center of the underworld and the heart of the empyreal sphere. A creature that does both simultaneously whilst roiling beneath the toiling waves of the ocean."

I stepped back. Dude used the word "whilst." Another very un-Miamian move.

"It's the serpent that lives in the water, that marks the equator, not dead but dreaming, the tip of its tail in its fang-filled jaws. When it awakes, it will drown this city."

Just then, Lisa stormed past.

"David, are you on break?"

"No."

"This isn't the time for personal conversations."

"He's a customer."

"If you've finished helping the customer, we need you in the back room. A shipment of books just arrived."

She hustled past, her hair helmet swinging like a clock pendulum on speed.

I wanted to talk more to this guy. He told me his name was Juan. He said he'd be in the cafe, reading.

I wanted to ask him about that guitar.

• • •

Heading towards the front of the store, ready for my second government-mandated 15 minute break of the day, I knew where Juan was before I saw him.

"Avast, me hearties!"

I walked through the cookbooks and saw him sitting at a table by the window. His red scarf, retied entirely so it covered his hair like a turban, stuck up from behind the book's cover. His guitar sat in the chair next to him, resting on its triangular base.

He was being heckled.

"I always see that fucking guy on campus."

"The Bon Jovi dude? He's in one of my classes. We call him Juan Bon Joker."

Juan didn't seem to notice them.

A falsetto rang out:

"I'm a cowboy . . . a ukulele on my back. . . ."

It was hard to ignore them. Most of the other people in the cafe looked up from their books.

"Hair stylist's been on strike . . . he's down on his luck ...."

The entire crew broke into peals of laughter. And Juan kept reading, his book a day-glo shield. How could he deal with it?

I asked Abel, the guy working the cafe, for a cup of coffee.

He told me about a show his band would be playing at some warehouse later in the week. I said I'd try to make it, if anything to check out the ladies the postpunk or indie rock or whatever you want to call it tends to bring out of the woodwork. Abel kept me at the counter, asking me about Claire. He wanted to know if he had a shot with her.

By the time I got my coffee milked and sugared, the hecklers had left, leaving behind a stack of magazines. Juan was still there, engrossed in his book. One of the women on the cover handed an eye to a guy with long hair. It made me think of the three witches in *Clash of the Titans*. The snake looked like it was creeping up behind the guy, ready to strike.

Juan set the book down, a wide grin stretched from ear to hells belled ear.

"He says we should read speech, sounds even, as images from the Triple Goddess."

I was more concerned about the dudes who'd been harassing him. I mean, it made sense, I suppose. I told you what he was wearing. Maybe you can get away with that kind of kit in some rusticated realm far in the Northern hemisphere—people would just think you're a historic reenactor, or some back to nature type. Maybe part of some fringe Mennonite group.

But here? Just try to imagine it: you finally splurged on that trip to South Beach you've been planning. Everyone at home's shoveling snow. Or at least sprouted a winter coat of fleece and five pounds of extra fat from sucking down those nut-encrusted cheese balls they've got at every holiday party. You, you're sitting at a sidewalk cafe on Ocean Drive. Throngs of people flood the sidewalk.

Across the street, beachside, a camera crew films for a commercial, or maybe a cop show, you guess. Crockett and Tubbs, guns ablaze, leap out of a yellow Testarossa parked in the sand. And there, leaning against a palm tree, some Tony Montana doppelgänger tosses back a mojito, throws the empty glass in the sand, and pulls a Glock out of the waistband of his white linen pants. Just as the two cops close in on the kill, a shambling pirate-boy, a pint-sized Captain Morgan, his skin as brown as spiced rum, cuts onto the scene, calling them all charlatans and fools. You can tell this guy's not in the script.

Very un-Miami. He fit in even less than I did, which seemed like a huge achievement. I guess that's why I went out of my way to talk to him.

I sat down and asked him, "Dude, do you know those guys?"

He explained they were in his classes at the local university. I felt a brief twinge of loserhood. Was everyone but me in college?

"I'm fine. It doesn't bother me. They're idiots. Simians, really."

"But even . . . I mean, 'Juan Bon Joker'? That's pretty harsh, man."

"What do I care? I hate them more than they hate me. No, even more than that. You know what? I don't even consider their existence. When I'm in class with them, I feel like we're having two completely different experiences. They're like primates, barely aware of the meaning of what they're reading. They're like, in *Moby Dick*, Queequeg, the savage. They don't know what's going on. But you know, that's not even right. It gives them too much credit. Queequeg is noble, he knows and experiences stuff that Ishmael knows nothing about. They're not like any character in any book you'd want to read because they have nothing to them. You know, when I was sitting there, of course I heard them. I'm not deaf. And they don't just call me after that Bon Jovi guy. They have another name for me, but one I actually like because it explains the difference between me and them. You know what it is?"

I had no idea. I looked from his bandana to his frilly smock to his knee high moccasins. Captain Shelley Running Bull? Who could say.

"The Bard. That's the newest one."

I had to stifle my laughter. That would have been my

second guess. College guys—you had to give it to them for ingenuity.

"The Bard. Like I'm some fucking minstrel decked out for their amusement. I like it. It spells out the difference between me and them. You see those fucking magazines over there? Pop music magazines. Men's magazines. 'How to' manuals for their empty lives. And you know where they were going after they left the bookstore? The fucking mall."

He pointed at my mug.

"Do you get those for free?"

After I got him a cup of coffee—technically forbidden for nonemployees, but Abel was cool and Lisa rarely came into the cafe—we started talking music.

4. Where the Nameless One Sleeps

That phrase Juan had used, "not dead but dreaming," I knew it well. I bet you know it too. That, or some variation, is in like a million songs. Metallica used it on "The Thing That Should Not Be." There's a Deicide song. Liers in Wait. Edge of Sanity. Even goths, like Fields of the Nephilim, are clued in to the mythos of the elder gods.

It's in a Valhalla song, too, "Where the Nameless One Sleeps." What's a metal album without an invocation to Cthulhu? Our muse in its tentacled form. I thought about the song as I piloted my crappy Pontiac Sunbird south on US1, headed from my Coral Gables apartment to the swampy, hurricane ravaged neighborhood where I'd grown up. Cutler Ridge. You might have seen our mall, swarming with looters, on TV. It hadn't been so long since Cthulhu had tried to annex the place as a subdivision of R'lyeh, the city where the nameless one sleeps. Not dead but dreaming.

If H.P. Lovecraft had owned a snowbird get-away, it would have been here. Too bad he's not dreaming, but dead. The neon luster of the rest of the city evaporates like rain on summer asphalt the farther south you drive. Stucco mansionettes and Italianate villas give way to cinderblock boxes fronted by stunted palm trees. And then you're in the Ridge. Its denizens have the same slack jawed stare as the amphibian townies in Lovecraft's tales. It's a multicultural Innsmouth. With gangsta flava.

John and Phil were driving back to Tallahassee that morning. I had the day off, and wanted to talk to them again about salvaging our band. I wanted to tell them about my talk with Sean. The tour. The contract. New Year's Eve came and went and I hadn't seen any of them since that one time John came by the store.

I kept thinking about that song, "Where the Nameless One Sleeps," even though, tape player busted, I drove along half listening to a Bad Company rock block on the radio. You can find an early version on the *Zombichrist* demo and a fully produced rendition on *Thrones of Satanic Dominion*. The label guys even put an ultraraw rehearsal take of the track on a promotional compilation shortly before they released *Thrones*. That song was about as close as we came to a hit single. It was like a death metal "Summer of '69."

The album cut starts with a batrachian choir of reverbed bullfrogs. A sample recorded in John and Phil's backyard, true, but meant to evoke the elder gods' demihuman disciples. The riff and the vocals begin together, puncturing the intro's murky croaks: "I am from the swamp/ where the nameless one sleeps."

I'd originally written the lyrics for a school assignment, around the time we'd started the band. It was one of our first songs. The teacher, Ms. Smith, gave the class a poem, called "Where I'm From," and asked us to write our own autobiographical rendition. We were supposed to, she said, Asian print skirt flowing as she flitted across the front of the classroom, "explore our identities."

In the original, George Ella something or other went on about the backwoods, how she's from clothes pins and fried corn. How she's from beet-flavored dirt that she ate. Reading the poem, I thought about the backwoods of my neighborhood, the strip of "woods" separating our subdivision from Biscayne Bay. You'd probably die if you ate the silty mud where the houses end and a dank mangrove swamp takes over. Much later, after the hurricane, the newspaper reported that the entire subdivision had once been swamp. It wasn't that the sea had swallowed the houses, it was more like the sea had only lended the land. Payback's a bitch.

My poem landed me in a parent/ teacher conference.

• • •

Ms. Smith, my parents, and I sat in her office, a small room carefully decorated with international knick knacks culled from a Pier 1 clearance sale. A batik cloth covered the desk. A row of wooden Buddhas stood watch over the computer keyboard. African masks and paper scrolls splashed with Japanese writing adorned the walls.

"Mr. and Mrs. Fosberg, I asked you to come in because I'm a little concerned about David."

She'd lined up her evidence next to the Buddhas: the original poem, my unholy rendition, and a copy of *Lord of the Flies*.

She explained the assignment, went on at length about the concept of identity. She showed them the original poem. My dad fidgeted, crossing this leg, then that. He leaned back in the seat, then perched on its front ledge. My mom, unmoving, stared blankly at the teacher. They'd come straight from work.

"Read it for yourself," Ms. Smith said as she slid mine across the desk.

I am from the boar's head equinox,
From black candles and chalk circles.

I am from the swamp where the
Nameless One sleeps
(Black flies buzzing,
It hung from a tree.
Black, hanging from a tree,
Its voice buzzed like
Raging flies.)

I am from the cotton Ceiba, the silkwood,
The Santero's sacred tree
Whose spiked trunk pricks
I remember
As portals beneath the flesh.

They finished reading. I sat, arms crossed, behind them. Indignant. I'd followed the assignment. I'd written about a memory. A childhood memory. Sure, I'd cast it in metal's mystic steel, but it was a memory all the same. Phil knew. He'd been with me.

My dad cleared his throat, then said "It looks like a poem. What's the problem with it?"

"Don't you see? He has to have made this up. Plus, that's a central image in a famous novel, *The Lord of the Flies*, which he read last year." Her middle finger plonked down on the leaf crowned boy on the book's cover.

"I checked with his teacher, Ms. Willis. More importantly, he's not writing about his identity, which is . . ." she paused, hoping my parents would fill her in.

They just glared at her.

"Identity is about personal discovery. I don't want to offend anybody, but this isn't David's identity. I mean, what can he possibly know about the Afro-Caribbean religious traditions he refers to? What can he know about Santeria? I believe he is belittling and demonizing another culture, a beautiful culture with much to offer."

My dad scoffed, but didn't say anything. Even he knew a thing or two about Santeria. There's a botanica, a kind of mystic Walgreen's, next to the DMV. We parked in front of it when I got my license. You can buy a spirit talisman to help you pass the driving test. When he saw that, he said, "No wonder the damn Cubans can't drive."

The local news, moreover, had recently run a series on people sacrificing chickens in their yards. The only things you should sacrifice in your yard, my dad thought, were weeds. With pesticide.

"Dad—that's true. I saw it in the woods when I was little."
Ms. Smith cut me off.

"He seems to have changed in the past year or so. I'm concerned that he's not really focused on the right things. That he's internalized some of the more fantastic elements of—" she looked around the room, as if the little Buddhas on her desk, the African masks on her wall, would mouth the right words, "*that music.*"

My mom, so grimly Teutonic, cold and steely, said with no trace of humor, "You mean the belching music."

And here, my dad, a little bit of a clown, let out a wild belchish roar, sustained it like Lee Dorian from Napalm Death, "*Buuurghhh!* How's that, David? Can I sing in your band?"

My mom smiled, very slightly. I understood even then that he had to work overtime to make her happy.

It threw Ms. Smith off guard. Before I knew it, I was in the back seat of the car and we were headed home.

My mom turned to me and said, "You do what that moon unit tells you to do."

They both seemed to think I was making fun of Santeria. That my poem was, to use my Dad's phrase, "a put on." I tried explaining what I'd seen, the swamp, the hold that memory had on me. That the music somehow explained it all. Just like a novel or a poem.

My dad, clearly sick of this, thirsty for his daily scotch and water too, sighed, "I've told you to tone it down, son. The belching music, the long hair, the death's heads on your shirts. Right or wrong, people judge you—" his hand shot off the steering wheel and stopped just inches from my nose. He snapped his fingers, "like *that.* Remember when you were in the second grade?"

My mom chimed in, "You wrote a story about a video game. It was that one. . . ."

"The one with flying ostriches. So stupid, these things," my dad added.

"They had us in there because the character died at the

end."

"And when you were in preschool, too. We've had a time with you kids."

"They said you were retarded. Couldn't color right. I told them you colored fine at home. The dingbats, they kept putting the crayons in your right hand."

I come from an unbroken line of lefties. My mom's one, too.

"And your sister?"

My dad, quick to make a joke, quipped, "Well, she *is* a little retarded."

"Maybe so. Living in that house they can't afford."

And from there, the plagiarized Santeria parody forgotten, they moved to a discussion of my sister's most recent foibles, which turned even the loudest belching music into a tiny whisper.

• • •

I turned off US1 and, on the side streets, noticed the scars left by the storm, even now, two years later. My parents moved across the country last year.

"We're going somewhere without hurricanes," they'd said.

I passed vacant houses with insurance company names spray painted on the garage doors. I nudged the car through intersections without traffic signals. There were no street signs. Or any landmarks at all. The trees we used to climb— ficus trees with twisted vines and trunks as thick and solid as brontosaurus toes—had long since been cleared away. I guided the car more by muscle memory than anything else. God knows how the pizza guy gets the job done.

I took the back entrance into our subdivision. On the right, a few houses showed signs of life—a new coat of paint here, a carefully trimmed hedge there. Envelopes and flyers sticking from the mouths of manatee- and dolphin-shaped mailboxes.

On the left, a mangrove swamp stretched to the curb. If you peered into the gnarled branches, you'd make out countless ropy roots arcing into a limitless expanse of shallow brown water. Even in Miami, you'd be hard pressed to find a developer with the cojones to gamble on that side of the street.

As I drove past the mangroves, the rotten-egg scent of the swamp instantly suffused the car and took me back to the second grade. Phil and John and I used to explore these woods every day. I'd known the Morris brothers since elementary school. When "heavy metal" meant plastic swords.

"Black flies buzzing, it hung from a tree," that's the line right before the guitar solo.

One second grade afternoon, it was just Phil and me out there. John wasn't with us—I think he was sick or something. After that day, Phil and I tethered ourselves to the Atari for a few months. Whenever John pestered us to go out into the woods, we'd blow him off, tell him we wanted to set a new high score for Joust.

Phil remembered, too. He had to. That's why this band implosion didn't make any sense. If I could talk to him, I thought, maybe we could work it out. We'd been marked from an early age. Taken the wrong path through the forest. Together. We'd been told to avoid the mangroves, but no one was there to stop us. Both my parents worked, Phil and John's mom, too. One of the neighbors, a drug cop, told my dad they'd seized like a ton of coke from an abandoned speedboat, just floating off the coast. At night, helicopters circled.

That one day, Phil with a pirate cutlass, me with a knight's rapier, we splashed along the trail, an obstacle course of 2 x 4s, plywood scraps, and packing pallets winding through the mangroves before meeting a flat, dry path that led to the bay.

You could find all kinds of cool things out here. Discarded welding tools doubled as maces. Soggy magazines—*Playboy* and *Penthouse*—flopped against piles of limestone rocks revealed strange mysteries in pop-up relief. Gentle tufts of mold crowned the mildewed blots of hairy beavers stretched across the pages. Like a children's book. Pat the bunny.

Sometimes you'd come across brown glass vials the width of a AA battery. If you screwed off their lids, you could see the crystalline flakes of some wizard's powerful potion.

That day, we'd gone a long way. We were close to the beach. The air stank of algae and motorboat fuel.

The mangroves gave way to scrawny oaks choked by bushy swarms of Brazillian pepper. As we neared the bay, we passed through stands dominated by Australian pines. Chunks of driftwood clogged together. Cicadas buzzed their constant song. We'd never been this far before, and saw a tree by the trail's edge that was different from all of these trees. Every branch, the entire trunk, was covered in thick spikes. If it were a person, the tree would be a heavily bullet-belted Rob Halford. Each spike, about a half inch long, was as sharp as a needle. I poked one and a single drop of blood beaded on my fingertip.

"Now this would make a good sword," John said and we circled the tree, looking for a downed branch. That's when we saw it. Something the size of a dog—a mastiff or an overfed terrier—hung from the trunk.

A boar's head, lashed to the tree with a buoy. The cicada song ebbed and we heard the flies, thousands of them, swarming around the boar's eyes, ears, and mouth. A pool of thick black blood coagulated on the ground. Flies spilled out of the jagged gash of a neck, as though the head was hollow, a flyhive of flesh.

We didn't hear a voice. No one fell into an epileptic fit. We felt no urge to bludgeon one another with conchs. This is not a supernatural tale.

We stood and stared. The flies buzzed around our heads too, looking to colonize our skulls, fill them with eggs.

Scuffling through the leaves, backing down the path, I stumbled over a stack of pennies. I looked around and saw similar stacks, plastic bowls of water, multicolored beads, arranged around the tree, the head. A single red flower floated in a paper cup by my foot.

Walking in, we'd ignored all this stuff, all these offerings, mistook them for the junk littering the woods. Half the trail's made of construction trash, remember?

"Look at that thing," I heard Phil, his plastic sword drawing a shaky line in the gravel as he ambled backwards. He turned and ran. The patter of Velcro sneakers against the plywood path raced like my heartbeat.

Backing away from the boar's head, backing away from the spiked boughs of the Ceiba tree, backing away from the piles of coins and Dixie cups set out to demarcate a wide half circle around the trunk, I saw that the boar's head hadn't been randomly set on the tree. Backing away, no longer able to see the chunky blood soaked tufts of gray fur, it looked like the head came out of the tree trunk, right where it split into three heavy, thorned limbs.

Sucking my pricked finger, I sprinted to catch up to Phil.

• • •

A Rush rock-block followed Bad Company as I pulled up to the Morris house, a low slung ranch painted a pale yellow. The front porch smelled a little mildewy, but other than that, none too worse for wear, considering the hurricane left a still-visible water line just inches below the ceiling. An older guy, sunburned and flat-topped, opened the door. He wore a striped golf shirt tucked into a pair of brown dress pants. He looked like Freddy Krueger, ready for a day on the links. He glared at me and made a face, like he'd just stepped in dog shit. He kind of "harrumphed," turned his head, his neck muscles tensed like cables, and shouted down the hall, "Some faggot here to see you girls!"

He stood there, like a doorman, then shook his arm at me.

"Well, come in already."

I stepped past him, my hands in fists at my side. It felt like he could pounce, at any moment and for any reason. I'd been here so many times before, but had never felt this kind of tension in the house. I headed to John's room. A bin teetering with clothes sat in the hall next to a few milkcrates packed with supplies: jumbo packs of toothpaste, pair after pair of blinding white socks, gallon-sized jugs of mouthwash. They were going to be gone for awhile.

John jammed a stack of t-shirts into a pink and blue Vidal Sassoon duffel bag.

"Hey, David."

"Nice bag, man."

"Yeah, I know. From the Miami Vice days. Makes me remember those cheesy white jackets we had. It's the only bag I've got left."

"Who's the drill sergeant?"

"Mom's new boyfriend, Greg." Their mom had cycled through a series of boyfriends in the time I'd known them. None of them had ever answered the door.

"Soon to be step dad. This summer. Why else," he gestured at his bed. It strained under a pyramid of milk crates, duffel bags, and backpacks, "do you think we're going to cram all this in the Honda?"

Phil came down the hall, carrying another laundry crate. Above the stack of laundry, I could see his curly, shoulder length hair. Greg followed behind, in lockstep, practically pushing Phil down the hall through the force of his hostile nagging. You could tell he wanted them out of the house.

"I thought you said you'd be gone by noon."

"Yeah?"

"It's past noon."

"I know."

"You're running late. You need to get on the road."

Phil set the crate on the bed and turned.

"Okay. I said 'I know.'"

This was enough to set Greg off.

"Don't you talk back to me, hotshot."

When he said the word "hotshot," he kind of stabbed Phil in the chest with his index finger. Twice. Once for each syllable. I thought they were going to fight. Instead, Greg stomped out of the room. Within moments, the TV blared in the other room.

Phil sang, under his breath, "*We got to get out of this place . . .*"

John finished the line, "*If it's the last thing we ever do.*"

I didn't stay too long after that. I drove, slow and leisurely, up Old Cutler Road to Merrie Christmas Park in Coconut Grove. I often went there on my off days. It's a little respite from all the concrete. At one point, the whole city must have looked like this, hammock islands separated by mangroves and sawgrass. The Timuqua or whatever giving praise to the sea. An old stand of ficus trees, like the ones we used to have in our yard, sprawled their brachiating branches down the side of a shallow ravine. I sat on the rippling wave of a branch-cum-root, it was hard to tell which came first, the warm sun slowly roasting me.

I couldn't really blame John and Phil. There were forces in this world more powerful than Cthulhu's suctioned grasp.

5. So Shall It Be

My visit to the park put me in a languid mood that stretched into a solitary evening in the apartment. I stood in the kitchenette, a cramped cubby about the size of two linoleum tiles, and poured cold Prego on noodles I'd just boiled, using their heat to warm the sauce. Spaghetti a la Bacchelori. I hoisted a gallon jug of Paisano wine off the counter and filled a Plutonic Records coffee mug reserved just for this purpose. A lavender husk of dried wine coated the bottom of the cup. By the time I get to the bottom, some flecks will dislodge. I'll chew them like scraps of a Fruit Roll-Up, then get a refill. Happens every night, except when I head to the bar.

I carried my pasta and wine into my room, a beige chamber indistinguishable from any other place I could afford except for the single luxury of a sliding glass door and balcony looking out onto the Coral Gables city hall, a limestone building that looked like it belonged on some sun scorched city square in Granada. At night, its ancient-seeming clock tower illuminated my window, making me think, at least for a moment or two, that I was in Granada, that I was somewhere exotic and distant.

Coral Gables, with its hacienda-style mansions and mango-hued sidewalks, seems an unlikely place for a death metal guitarist to live, you might think, but the apartment offered a few key advantages: first, before the devastating break up that has, at least temporarily, led me to swear off women in a Morrissey-like attempt at celibacy, I lived within walking distance of my girlfriend, whose well-off parents thrived in this environment of wealth and privilege. Second, I also lived a short walk from the Crown and Garter, a British pub with Guinness on tap and on special. Third, I lived a short drive from Yesterday and Today, a record shop with the largest selection of metal in South Florida. I said earlier you'd have to special order our album at most music stores, but they always stocked a few copies.

The apartment was filled with promo items like the cup. CDs, LPs, and tapes filled a row of shoeboxes set on the floor. Half of them were promos sent from the label. I'd plastered the wall by my bed with promo posters. A stack of free shirts, some for Valhalla, some for other groups on the Plutonic roster, teetered on a wire shelf. Sometimes, I sold stacks of promo CDs at the used music shop by work, a habit that probably added about an extra tenner a week to my GDP.

I wondered if I would miss all this crap when I wasn't in a band. I pulled another shoebox—this one crammed with zines, letters from tape traders, and flyers from record labels even more obscure than Plutonic, from under the bed. Why did I keep them?

I flipped through the envelopes, the postmarks printed in a dozen languages, the stamps of everything from Slavic kings to insects of the Amazon. I kept them because they reminded me of two things: 1. the world was out there, a wide ranging thing that could never be trapped by the daily tedium of a minimum wage slave and 2. I had, at least through the magnetized appendage of a tape, through the miracle of sound encased in vinyl and plastic, managed to touch that world.

The good reviews were like little love poems I'd hold onto forever. I flipped through several I'd cut out from magazines after we'd released the first album. I pulled out the bio sheet Plutonic had sent out with all the promo copies of *Thrones of Satanic Dominion*. It was written in this overblown style that clearly overemphasized our importance. I knew that, but I liked to read it when I felt down. The photo at the top of the bio sheet showed us standing on the swollen python roots of the Merrie Christmas ficus where I'd spent the afternoon. With his shaved head, Budweiser shirt, and knee length surf shorts, Jake looked like he'd just finished mowing the yard. Phil looked the most put together, almost airbrushed. His hair hung around his shoulders in loose ringlets. He wore a black silk shirt and pointy toed boots. If I remember right, he'd just come from a gig with the school jazz ensemble at some ritzy wine bar. John and I stood between Jake and Phil; we looked like brothers, both with equally lank, long brown hair, him in a long sleeved Obituary t-shirt, cut off camouflage shorts, and Reebok hi-tops and me wearing jeans and a t-shirt you can't read because my arms are crossed. Below that, there was the track listing for the album and a few paragraphs of copy designed to get college radio stations to play it and record shops to buy it.

The first Valhalla full length album, *Thrones of Satanic Dominion*, is upon you. This essential force of Florida death metal distills the genre to its essence. It's true that quite a number of death metal bands have come out of Florida recently, and Valhalla have taken that approach and maximized its potential. Muscular riffs thunder from intro to outro on this essential release. Each well-placed solo, brief and frantic, slashes like a blade through water. The vocals pronounce the end, proclaim the imminent arrival of a zombified messiah. The drums thunder like the ravages of a category 5 storm.

Valhalla formed in Miami in 1989. The members went to the same high school and have known each other since they were kids. Phil and John got the other guys into metal. "One of our Mom's boyfriends left some AC/DC tapes at the house, and it just kind of escalated from there," says John. "That guy was a dick, but I guess he did one thing right. Phil got a guitar as a Christmas present and it wasn't too long before I was playing it, too." Of the band, David has more of a classical background. "I started playing piano when I was, like, six. I'd say J.S. Bach inspired me more than Sebastian Bach when I was a kid. Still, Phil and John always shared music with me and, by about 8th grade, I started to catch on. I transitioned to guitar. My parents still haven't forgiven me." "I grew up listening to Two Live Crew," drummer Jake deadpans when asked about his influences. "There's not a lot of options. It was this or marching band."

Valhalla put out their first release, the *Zombichrist* EP, by themselves. Released on 666 hand numbered cassettes, the EP soon captured the attention of the underground. And of a number of churches in Florida, who continue to protest at shows and burn albums by death metal bands. A review in *Cerebral Holocaust* praised it as "a godly assault of brutality." Even *Cardiac Arrest*, known for their critical acumen, exclaims that "the songs are . . . blindingly fast." The new album promises a deepening of the sound that comes as Valhalla has matured as a band.

Their live shows are not to be missed. If you have the chance to see Valhalla in concert, you should be careful when you hear the opening chords of "Zombichrist." By the time they get to the chorus, the repetitive ritualistic barrage of a

triple-vocal attack on the resurrection,
the crowd erupts, the mosh pit like a
seething whirlpool:
On the cross, he drinks the potion—
Zombichrist
Culled from creatures of the ocean—
Zombichrist
Prepare the spinefish paste, fish for
men—Zombichrist
No resurrection, undead rises again—
Zombichrist.

Valhalla represents Florida death metal
at its peak. The songs evoke power
through their alteration of Maiden
inspired speed and hardcore influenced
rhythms. After opening for Bolt Thrower
on the opening night of their first US
tour, Valhalla garnered the attention of
representatives from a number of the top
labels in the underground. Luckily, they
chose Plutonic, and we're proud to offer
you their first full length release,
Thrones of Satanic Dominion.

To arrange interviews and booking
information, contact Sean at (xxx) xxx-
xxxx. Tracks to highlight include:
Track 1: Where the Nameless One Sleeps
Track 3: Zombichrist
Track 7: Dead Cities Slumber Beneath the
Waves

What would happen to all this stuff? I thought. Valhalla was
done. I looked at my watch. John and Phil must be about
midway through the state by now, pulling past pastel south
Florida and into the mossy woodlands of north Florida.
Already, just a year after the album's release, the ads in
magazines like *Kerrang!* and *Metal Hammer* had ceased.
Admittedly, they'd been microscopic, black and white, and
wedged firmly between shills for "water pipes" and discount

amps. The reviews and mail had slowed to a trickle.

I don't want you to get the wrong impression. Not everything in the box was sweetness and light, unvarnished praise for my guitarmanship. In the tiny world of death metal, I did not reign as king. And some of the things in this box reminded me of that, too. There were plenty of negative reviews by self-righteous scenesters, zine producing obsessive compulsives drawn by the cataloguing possibilities unleashed by metal's profusion of subgenres: this is blackened death doom tinged by a gothic sensibility while that is clearly goth rock referencing classic doom through blackened death atmospherics.

I pulled out one of the worst, a review of our *Zombichrist* demo by some guy from Fort Lauderdale, Martin Rosenbaum, a prog rock purist who somehow had a soft spot for early Napalm Death-style grindcore. He had no tolerance for anything in between. He specialized in negative publicity, particularly when it came to Florida style death metal:

Cardiac Arrest Reviews

Valhalla. Zombichrist. 4-track demo.
Four songs. No label.

Man, what a piece of excretious offal! When I think of derivative Florida-style death metal, I will now think of Valhalla from Miami. All of the generic and repetitive features of this style of "music" are firmly in place, the most prominent being the continuous belch of the vocalist. This is my least favorite part of all of these bands—I wish they would wake up and give the proper respect to real bands, like Dream Theater, Yes, or Rush. Valhalla will never reach anywhere close to greatness. On second thought, they'd probably be better off playing grindcore. Don't try so hard, guys! It's the pretensions of this kind of music that annoy me the most.

Besides the vocal "style," let's briefly look at the inane lyrics of the title track:

Roman soldiers defile, despise
Crush the cenotaph
Zombichrist rise

Is anyone really offended by this kind of anti-Christian lyric? The feeble blasphemy, paired with the inverted pentagram that they somehow managed to incorporate into the illegibile scrawl of their logo reminds me of exactly why I hate bands like this. You can just tell that these guys are dense and opaque losers. In fact, I can't believe they even have the nerve to send their demo to me in the first place. If they're from Miami, they should know that I don't suffer fools lightly.

I can't even believe they figured out how to hit "record" to commit this shit to tape. Besides their completely derivative and—I contest—unimaginative lyrics and vocal delivery, their drummer completely lacks any dimension. The songs are either blindingly fast, with continual double bass, or the almost stand-still bare bones rhythms of the mosh parts. In fact, I can imagine these guys cheering to their own songs as they slam dance in their mommies' living rooms. The worst part of this demo, and that's saying a lot once you've read the lyrics to their paean to the so-called greenhouse effect, "Dead Cities Slumber Beneath the Waves", I mean, look at these inane lines:

Icy flow of glacial melt
Oceans consume equatorial belt
Buildings topple beneath the waves
Cries for help, but no one saved

When a prog rock band tackles a social issue, it makes sense; thoughtful lyrics go with thoughtful music. But who do these guys think they are? Midnight Oil? Whew, I got a bit carried away. I'm starting to get chest palpitations just thinking of how much I hate this demo. The worst thing, and I can't forget this because it grieves me deeply as a fan of real guitarists, is the complete thievery and lack of respect for real bands so unembarrasedly on display on this completely unpromising demo. When I think of dual guitar harmonies, I think of two bands—Iron Maiden and Mercyful Fate. Notice that I did not mention Valhalla in that last line. These guys shamelessly steal all of the tricks and techniques of the aforementioned gods. The only plus side to this outright plagiarism is you can barely hear the guitar playing on the demo anyway, what with the cookie monster vocals, downtuned bass fart, and the continuous drum solo. The whole thing sounds like a pack of wild dogs afflicted with diarrhea. Fart. Bark. Repeat. Ad nauseum.

Hey guys—do the right thing—stop this madness, and send an apology letter to me, and to the true metal bands you rip off daily. I'd suggest you send a letter apologizing to your fans, too, but I can't imagine you actually have any.

--Martin

And then there are the death threats, which aren't many, but stick with you. The music, I suppose, impels them. Although, that said, these did not seem to be written by fans, unless the concerned congregants of the Pentecostal church in Clearwater, for example, bought twenty copies of *Thrones* for some purpose other than burning them in the parking lot at one of our shows. Apparently, there's even some kind of form letter, a death threat template, employed by the righteous because I have identical letters pronouncing damnation through the same scripture laden style, with postmarks pockmarking the I-4 corridor.

I received the most recent one just last week. It was a bit different in that it hadn't been penned by some aspiring missionary eager to cast *Thrones* into an end time drama foretold by the book of Revelations. Whoever wrote it liked metal. Liked it enough to run a record label. We just didn't play the right kind of metal.

The envelope hadn't yet made it into my box of mementoes. It sat next to Juan's number on top of two milk crates stacked together to form a bedside table. Unlike the church penned threats that started by telling me my soul was a precious lamb, a feather floating through the expanse of eternity, this one got right to the point:

I write this as I cast a spell of destruction upon each member of your band.

May boils cover your vocal cords. So shall it be.

May warts encrust your playing fingers. So shall it be.

Death Metal Epic I: The Inverted Katabasis

May rheumatisms spasm your hands. So shall it be.

By opening this letter you have unleashed the breath of centuries, the breath of curses,
that I breathe into your faces. I write to wish you

Death
Death
Death

And yet you shall never know death. Not truly. Your death metal does not deserve the name.

Here, at least, was a place where this guy and Martin Rosenbaum were in agreement.

You make life metal. You do not know death, with your songs about environment, about politics, about the meaningless tragedies of this world. You do not know death, as you stand in your band photo wearing basketball shoes and swimming shorts. In reality, you care about banalities, about getting laid and doing right. You do not make death metal. You make life metal and you will never truly know the utter power of total death. You will thank me when my curse wreaks *havoc upon you. You will praise my name as you cry with spasms of disease. So shall it be. And yet, even though you will know death intimately, you will yet be life metal. For while you cry out against death, total death metal cries for its emptiness, total death metal cries out in its own infinite empty empty silence. Your life metal is no match for deaths despondent abyss.*

After all that, he'd included a polite salutation, signing off "Yours, Nekrokor." Some evidence of this "curse" lingered at the bottom of the envelope. There were a few stones marked with runic inscriptions in white chalk, a black fabric patch of a pentagram that suffered from what looked like chemical burns, and a paste of greenish sludge wedged into the folds and crevices of the envelope. I'd held onto the envelope, despite the green sludge, which, on second thought, maybe wasn't the best idea. It included a return address, printed on a little sticker like the kind my mom uses for paying bills, but instead of a name and address and a picture of, like, a butterfly or a blue jay, this Nekrokor guy had a return address sticker with his name printed like a band logo:

The name for his record label, Despondent Abyss, came next, followed by an address of a PO Box somewhere in Europe.

Too late, "Nekrokor," I thought, as I headed back to the kitchen for a Paisano refill. How could he kill something that was already dead?

6. Metametal: A Dream of the Nekronomikon

Book of the Dead
Pages bound in human flesh
Feasting the beast
From the blood the words were said
I am unseen, dreamt the sacred passage aloud
Trapped in a dream of the Nekronomikon
—Deicide, "Dead by Dawn"

Like the darkened forest, I also wear a shroud, a black cloak. My bare feet crunch leaves underfoot as I step deeper into a shrouded vale. It is either dusk or early morning. A sharp luminescence frames and accentuates the sky, dark but glowing. A sliver of moon peers from above. I know it reflects the sun's light. It also absorbs the warmth from the earth. I move faster, unsure of my destination, but clearly aware of the path I must follow. The trees close in above me, forming a tunnel of textured, nearly serrated bark. Then, I come to a fork in the path. On the right, the trees thin, then give way to a well-worn village green. I hesitate, but only for the briefest instant. Above, the branches, like the gnawed claws of a wizened shaman, point irresistibly down the left-hand path.

And so I choose the left-hand path.

The sound of my feet pounding the ground resounds like a heartbeat, but muffled by the surrounding trees. The path descends, seemingly into the roots themselves. I maintain my pace, but now I hang in the air on every other step. I grow lighter as I venture deeper. Then, I only push against the ground at irregular intervals. Otherwise, I float, my toes pointing toward the ground.

Whatever lies at the end of this path now draws me with its power.

Ahead, the trail ends, extends into a circular alcove. Something bright hangs at the center. I float into the center of a hollowed sequoia. A witches' hollow, the inside a burnished orange like the flicker of a thousand jack o' lantern candles.

A hallowed hollow, the walls etched with an endless cascade of wood rings, marked over eons, each distinct impression its own saga of flood, flame, drought.

Now I hang before a pale rectangle. It also floats. It has the dimensions of a book—the Bible or an encyclopedia—but its flesh colored cover extends smooth and unbroken around the edges.

I reach out to touch it, warm and pulsing. Not entirely smooth, but covered in a soft fur, like baby down, springing, I notice, from tiny follicles around the entire book. If this were the moon, each follicle would be like the tiniest fist of a crater.

A sound suffuses the wooden cavern and at first I mistake it for the voice of the book. In this vision, the book will speak to me, revealing its hidden message, I think, and so I focus on its cover. A breeze shakes the leaves, and I hear the song, "Dead by Dawn," Glenn Benton's death grunt, "Book of the Dead … pages bound in human flesh," muted into the mumbling of cicadas, and repeating into an incessant susurrus, slurring into an indecipherable syrup of sound.

I am not fazed by this at all. The words define the moment, suffuse the air, and echo my thoughts on the only book powerful enough to draw my spirit being through the forest. Instead, floating in front of this book, a beacon outshining the moon and outpacing the sun, I consider the message, wonder how to read the forbidden words, how to decipher the deadly messages of the Nekronomikon.

Almost in answer to my thought, the next line of "Dead by

Dawn," each word a distinct but echoing groan, slowed to 15 rpm and amplified by 100 bass cannons, rolls into the tree cavern, like some monolithic beast seeking refuge.

"Feasting the Beast ... from the blood the words were said."

"Feasting the Beast." I mouth the words in a manner very different from the hundreds of times I've listened to the first Deicide album. There is no head banging, no air guitar.

Now the line is a clue, a puzzle. What is the Beast in this context? The book, or the forest? The sounds of the song itself? Some creature burrowing beneath? In the logic of the dream, I stare at the ground, note my bare feet with their long claw like nails hovering six inches above the forest floor, and remember the knife tucked into a pocket in my robe.

A knife.

And I've had it all along.

I pull it out and, to test its sharpness, poke my index finger. I squeeze a drop of blood onto the book, its cover as barren and luminescent as the moon above. The book absorbs my blood. The drop disappears and the humming, now indistinguishable as voices or insects, its source indistinguishable as well, intensifies. Is this thundering rattle emanating from Glenn Benton's calloused vocal cords? I mean, is he here, smoking Marlboro reds while on a midnight stroll? Or is the song streaming from some headphones hidden, along with the knife, in my monkish cowl?

But I understand. Such questions have no meaning. The forest hungers for more. The leaves twitter in anticipation. The moon's glow intensifies in the clearing. Its sliver is actually a slit. The branches cast a shadow, a figure, a five-pointed star, on the cover of the book. I poke the point of my knife into the top left corner of the cover.

Inhuman insect voices, the bass rumbling of sleeping worms, intone more Deicide lyrics:

"Levitate through the sacred and ancient doors ... levitate through the sacred and ancient doors."

I carve a pentacle into the cover. It bleeds, but absorbs the blood. The bloodred gash of the pentagram churns like a raging river. And at the center of the pentagram an additional wound—one I did not cut—opens, then closes, then opens again.

The wound reveals a blue eye, winking, turning, focusing, twisting, at the center of the book. The voices, dense layers of sound produced by innumerable jaws, mandibles, stomata, intones:

"Unseal the pages."

The eye, occasionally blinking, stares.

I slice slowly, the eye fixated on, following the path of, the blood soaked blade as it sears through infant flesh.

I finish, dropping the knife, which, unlike me, falls to the ground. Instantly, it sinks into the earth, drawn under by whatever creatures tunnel beneath the roots of these trees.

The eye blinks, then gazes at me, its pupil dilating to the edge of the iris, threatening to extend outward, to stain the flesh of the book dusky black. I open the cover. The book's eyelid flutters beneath my palm. Words like wounds read "Worship Me" in letters formed from razor gashes.

Terrified, I flip to another page, and then another.

The same bleak message, the same ornate script, pronounces its doom. My doom.

7. The Ouroborean Descent

The top hat, rescued from some musty Miracle Mile bridal shop, suffered from an all-encompassing case of mange. Patches of coarse black hair, like the fur of some oversized rodent, alternated with barren expanses of threadbare silk so worn they looked more gray than black. Above one ear, I could see two playing cards, the Joker and Queen of spades, wedged into the wide band of green and burgundy ribbon wound around the base of the hat. Six dead roses, pink and shriveled as baby kittens, peered from the other side of the brim. Beneath the brim, Juan grinned wide, a Cheshire cat or a mad hatter.

"Good to see you, man." He lifted a rust colored guitar as gnarled and battered as a sunken oil platform. "I brought the axe this time."

Gadgets, machinery, and industrial detritus covered its orangish gray body: I could make out clock gears, the wiry innards of a remote control or portable radio, a squat plastic box that looked suspiciously like a G.I. Joe jetpack. Three rusted razor blades superglued to the neck threatened tetanus with every tuning. It was the only guitar you could shave with.

I'd spotted him, the top hat, the guitar, the red velvet suit jacket he wore, from across the parking lot. I drove to the university from work. We'd agreed to meet after his night class, something on, fittingly enough, Renaissance poetry.

"I thought we could use the studio—my girlfriend works for the radio station—but she says there's a meeting or something in there tonight."

"There's a studio?"

"Yeah, but we'll have to use the music rooms tonight. They're always open."

We hauled our instruments across campus, passing packs of students, professors, and middle aged professionals who could have been either. We walked through the foyers and patios of buildings assembled from concrete girders as gray and solid as the underside of a highway bridge. We passed along abstract murals of glossy pastel tiles.

I followed Juan up a set of stairs and into a small white room outfitted with two school desks and a battered brown piano. I hadn't played a piano in some time, not since the hurricane warped ours into a useless hunk of driftwood, really not since I'd moved out on my own, but I'd played it for years before I learned the guitar.

I sat down at the bench and my hands immediately fell into a familiar position, the opening notes for Handel's "Sarabande," one of the few classical songs I still remembered, its mournful minor tone foreshadowing my eventual musical path. I played the first section of the song, using the pedal to transmute this baroque dance hit into a droning lament.

Juan plopped a leather satchel onto the top of the piano and started digging through it. Like Juan himself, it was covered in baubles and accessories: patches, coins, pins, even the mummified foot of a pygmy alligator. Around his neck, a small red plasticine hand with a hazel doll's eye embedded in the palm hung from a leather shoelace.

"The eye of Sauron," I said, nodding at it and improvising a doomy bass line with my left hand.

"Of course. And," he plunged into the bag, "I've got something that's going to totally guide us through Mordor."

He pulled out a thick book of orchestral music from Richard Wagner's *Siegfried* opera. A Booksalot 75% off sticker curled up from the front cover.

"I got this the day I picked up *The White Goddess*. I couldn't resist after our talk. Two dollars. It's like they are just giving it away."

I wanted to tell him there was no way I could play all of that.

He opened the book and set it on the piano's music stand. Annotations for different instruments—oboe, clarinet, timpani—ran down the left margin. Each page covered about five measures of a crushingly long and ornate opera. Juan had blocked certain measures with colored pencils—this oboe passage, that flute trill—and drawn arrows, up, down, forward, and backward, around selected sections.

"I know you're more of a musician than I am. Gale, my girlfriend, bought that Valhalla album for me after I told her about you. That's some pretty serious stuff. Fast. And the vocals—they reminded me of some goblin march, some Lovecraftian fish-choir. But if you'll hear me out, I think you'll agree I've found another way, a different way, to trek through the dark lands."

• • •

After practice, back at home, I couldn't sleep, even though I had the 6 AM opening shift. I sat cross legged on the floor in front of the Wagner book and a Casio keyboard I dragged out of the closet. I'd bought it in the third grade, but hadn't used it much since then, its limited range of polka beats and synthesized banjo sounds having long lost their allure. Now I looked at it differently, like its dusty, cramped keys could reveal a new sound. Juan had found another path through the dark lands, one founded on what I'd thought as the least metal-y instrument of all, the lowly synthesizer.

Sure, Juan couldn't play as well as Phil. As we played, the sounds undulated, slowly shifting tempo. Sometimes it took him a second to find the right note. But if we could structure and record what we'd done in the piano room, we could go far beyond anything I'd done with Valhalla. We'd be more than a good death metal band; we could change what death metal could sound like.

He'd marked the book in a way that seemed alchemical, that changed the opera into something new. We played measures he had marked with the same color. We played them repetitively and in seemingly random combinations. An up arrow meant we played some thunderous Wagnerian tetrachord as a sequence, starting with the bottom note. In some measures, he'd circled a few of the notes in one color, green, and a few more in another color, red. We first played the green series, then the red. I spent most of the night playing the piano, my foot on the echo pedal. The combination of piano and guitar created a shroud of sound. Juan didn't play guitar like a metal guy, either. Instead of a constant barrage of chords, he meandered through an odd, atonal series, only occasionally punctuated by anything riff-like.

"What are we going to do about drums?" I asked at one point.

"Modern music is so drum oriented. We should deliberately have no drums. Or, at most, some real percussion, like a kettledrum. I bet we can track one down."

I experimented with tones and speeds. Each measure contained at least one devastating riff, sometimes an entire song contained in a single moment. The trick was to salvage them, translate them. Even on the Casio, the sounds assumed a luminescent spectrality: the glockenspiel became a ghostly bell tolling, the vibraphone a stalled clutch on a Klingon cruiser. He said we'd definitely practice in the studio next time, that his girlfriend had a key, and that they had several keyboards with MIDI processors. If I could channel the spirits through a console piano, a Casio, then who knows what we could make if we secluded ourselves in the studio?

• • •

The work week melted into a familiar routine of working, not working while at work, and drinking to forget about work after work. Some nights, I'd sketch ideas into the Wagner book. I slipped sheets of paper with full song ideas—splotches of color more drawings than songs—between the pages. Next to colors, I listed page numbers of coordinating parts, the kinds of voices I wanted to use, and notes for a bass line to solidify the structure.

This time, when I saw him, Juan held up a key latched, like his Sauron hand, around his neck.

"No piano room tonight, my friend."

The studio was dark and cool, its interior kept at a constant temperature to keep the equipment from overheating. I made a mental note to bring a sweater next time. Juan adjusted the lights—recessed, on a dimmer—so that the room assumed the calm seriousness of a candle lit chapel at midnight. The studio had more than atmosphere; it also had the tools we needed to hone this new approach, even to record an album. A bank of graphics equalizers and speakers fronted one wall. We sat on leather office chairs at a console with pickups, sound meters, and recording equipment. A microphone stand occupied a corner of the room, its walls covered in sound dampening foam.

I turned on the keyboard and experimented with its settings. The room shook as bass tremors streamed from the massive amplifiers mounted to the ceiling in either corner. A shriek like a needle hitting vinyl cut in; Juan joined in on his guitar with high pitched pterodactyl tones. The back of my head tingled, the sounds massaging like some deluxe shower head.

We shared our ideas and played, without really stopping, for several hours. We took turns marking the Wagner book, explaining our notes. In the cocooned interior of the studio, the time passed like a single moment. I checked my watch: it was nearly midnight. We'd been there since seven.

Juan put his guitar down and rummaged through his leather satchel. His coins and doodads jangled like a cash register. He pulled out a sheet of paper and taped it to the wall facing the keyboard with a paint-stained strip of frayed duct tape. He'd put up a picture that looked like a tie-dyed fruit loop. I looked closer. A multicolored loop with tiny dragon wings? It was a serpent, looped, consuming its tail:

"That's the thing you talked about that day in Booksalot . . . for your tattoo."

"The Ouroboros. I painted this based on an etching of the creature found in the *Synosius* of the fifteenth century alchemist Theodoros Pelecanos."

I peered at it again. He'd colored each individual scale, from the thick octagonal scales on the creature's jade back to the light lavender layer shimmering across the dragon's belly. He was a good artist—I could make out individual fangs, the blue-green shading circling the sullen eyes, the solid skeletal structure underlying its arms. But I wasn't sure how to respond, what he wanted. Nice picture?

"I think we should do a song about it. Or, not about it, but a song that sounds like the Ouroboros. A tone poem, to use Wagner's phrase. More than that, I think the Ouroboros is a concept that should guide our playing, our recording. You know you can't always look at things like everyone else in this city, like some macho bro. This is a contemplative image. An image intended to evoke ritualistic contemplation. That's how alchemists used the image, as a means of evoking the transmutation of notes, sounds, the soul."

I listened as he explained. I hadn't thought what we were doing would be so different from Valhalla. I thought I'd find some new people and keep on where *Thrones of Satanic Dominion* left off. But as I listened, I realized Juan could never replace Phil, John, and Jake. And how could I expect him to? What he proposed was something different. Something deeper, even. We could make music that expressed a different emotion, still dark, but exulting that darkness.

If I hadn't spent the past few years playing Satanic death metal, I'd say we experienced a kind of spiritual communion, staring at his picture, finding tones that evoked the serpent's coils, contemplating the shifting form of the eternal dragon. I felt goosebumps on my arms and neck. Maybe I felt them *because* I'd spent the past few years in a death metal band, because of the Slaytanic past?

• • •

We stepped out of the studio with a rough mix of two expansive songs. The campus was empty, its silence magnified by its contrast to our hours of playing.

"What time is it?"

I looked at my watch; it was almost two.

"Shit. Gale must have left already. I told her I'd meet her here at ten. And I don't have a ride."

"Do you want me to give you a ride? I can drop you off."

"Yeah, thanks. She lives about ten minutes from here. If you could take me to Gale's, that would be great."

As we walked across campus, he asked me if I had a girlfriend.

"Ah man, I fucked up. I had the best girlfriend before I

started working at Booksalot. Gothy. Otherworldly. With long black hair, so thick you could lose yourself in it. No lie, it smelled like jasmine. On the first date, we were in some side alley in Coconut Grove. She said 'I think I might be a witch . . .' and that was it. I was fully in love."

"What happened?"

"Like I said, man. That job happened. Life. Struggling to pay the bills. It wasn't just that I worked all the time. I worked all the time and felt like a loser. She had no answers for me. She was mysterious, sure, but not super outgoing. She lived at home. Never had a job. Plus, I met all these girls at work. They were doing stuff. Going to school. Selling fucking real estate. Something. They were doing something."

He kind of winced.

"At first it was innocent enough. I just collected phone numbers. I never called them. It was more, like, the challenge. Easy, too, once the album came out. Felt like a store-brand rock star. Before you know it, I'm getting a little too close. It all ended. Then I realized how good I'd had it. They don't all, you know, smell like jasmine."

I caught myself. What was I doing? Unclasping the book of my secret soul? I sounded ridiculous, going on about the floral scent of my one lost love. I sounded as effeminate as Juan's costume, the things I was telling him as frilly as his smock. I hadn't even told this shit to Claire, who I could trust. Costumed or not, I thought, this guy's just another dude. Beneath the disguise, someone who could easily ridicule or take advantage of any perceived weakness. An adolescent dickhead, like me.

I spit on the ground, then changed my tone.

"For real, though. Some just smell. Some won't suck dick."

"I could have told you that."

"I didn't even consider it. Worst of all, none of them liked metal. I found myself trying to get play while listening to the Indigo Girls. So lame. I guess I'm just kind of over it right now."

"Did she *like* metal?" He sounded skeptical that this was

possible.

"Well, that was the thing. She totally got the emotion behind it. She didn't recoil. We didn't, like, get busy to Morbid Angel or anything. I think she understood it."

"Can you get back with her?"

"Oh, no way. I tried. She won't even talk to me."

"Well, you're not the only one with problems, my friend."

"Yeah? How so?"

"First, Gale will definitely be pissed about this. She must have banged on the door, and we didn't hear her. Let me just say that this is not unusual for me."

"So she's used to it, right?" I knew lots of guys who had found girls resigned to their bad behavior. I imagined any girl dating Juan would have to belong to that category.

"Less and less with each day. She's graduating soon and has started asking me about our plans for the future. I don't have plans for tomorrow, let alone some distant future of, you know, working endlessly at some job. I'm not geared to the industrial machine, like she is. She's even been buying new clothes—expensive stuff, black pant suits from Ann Taylor. She says they're for interviews and work, but I think they're like," he smirked, "'bard repellent'. She's serious about work, being a grown up, but I'm serious about this," he touched his top hat, jangled his necklace, "about my poetic profession. It's like Robert Graves says. The whole function of poetry, the purpose in this world, is religious invocation of the Triple Goddess, the Muse."

We got to my car. I unlocked the doors and loaded my instruments. I eased into the driver's seat and started the car. The razored neck of Juan's guitar swung past my eyes and nicked my ear. The four blades lodged themselves in the car headliner, unleashing an orange shower of foam. Juan, oblivious, one moccasined foot in the car, the other in the parking lot, wedged the blades deeper into the headliner.

"Stop, dude," I shouted, rubbing a drop of blood between my fingers. Somehow, Juan managed to get in the car and shut the door without breaking anything else. It would cost at least $100 to fix the ruined headliner, almost twenty hours of retail toil I thought, as I pulled out of the parking lot. We drove in silence broken only by his directions to Gale's house: "left here," "right on 107th," "turn right at this light." Foam rained from the gashes in the headliner at every stop, on every turn.

8. Escar-a-gogo

Juan never paid me for the headliner. For the next few months, it flapped in the wind and draped like a tattered wedding veil over the head of anyone unlucky enough to ride shotgun. He more than made up for it with his ideas, his energy, his complete obliviousness to what "counted" as metal for people like Martin Rosenbaum or Sean and Mike. For him, "metal" was an emotion, a feeling of connection with some past, some ancient entity not dead but dreaming. When we weren't playing, he assailed me with monologues on religion, art, and myth.

After I gave him a death metal mixtape: "I think I understand why these bands try to be so 'satanic.' The rift separating Christianity and poetry is a consequence of modern life—careers, reason, logic. It's pretty obvious that they are trying to create the ecstatic trance of the shaman, the bard, through an inversion, a reversal, of all the Christian formulas they know."

When I asked him what he was studying *to be*, you know, like job wise: "I am studying to be independent, at whatever cost, to think mythically as well as rationally so that I can fulfill my calling. I am seeking to limit my contact with all things that prevent one from being attuned to what really matters."

I asked him about Gale, who I still hadn't met. What was she like, how did they meet—that kind of thing. I had a hard time imagining what kind of girl would go for a guy like Juan, and it sounded like their relationship was on the rocks: "What kind of girl is Gale? David, I've been wondering the same thing myself. What is she like? I thought she was my muse, my queen, her pale skin like the moon, the white goddess." Had he been listening to Moonspell? I hadn't put them on the mixtape. "Now, though, I think she means to destroy me, devour me and leave me behind."

I don't think he ever asked me a single question, unless it was a rhetorical segue into another explanation of the significance of a song lyric. I went to the campus so much, I started to feel like a student. We practiced several nights a week. By the time the brief blip of Florida winter slipped into spring, we'd pieced together a few very long songs punctuated by two meditative soundscapes cobbled together from manipulated samples of insect chatter—clattering mandibles, cicadas buzzing—and a plush wash of extended chords.

We had become a different band. No blast beats. No mosh break downs.

We needed to finish recording something soon. I'd stopped answering the phone at home as Sean's messages grew more insistent and threatening. Sometimes, he'd just say, "The contract, David. Remember the contract," and then hang up. And our unlimited hours of recording were near their end. I knew it the night I first met Gale. Like usual, I went to meet Juan outside of the cafeteria. Students filled the picnic tables, eating and talking. The sunset colored everything in pastel shades. A group of guys stood in a circle kicking a hacky sack. In the middle of the sidewalk, Juan, today decked out like a top hatted monk in a purple robe cinched with a corded white belt, cowered as a tall, round woman glowered at him.

This, I could tell, was Gale. She had shoulder length brown hair and pink lipstick smeared well past her lips. More like mouthstick. She stood a head taller than Juan. With his top hat on, they were about even. I understood why Juan was threatened by her clothes; she aspired to, but had not yet mastered, the dull rigidity of businesswear. She wore a black Ann Taylor pantsuit, true, but the jacket seams hung well past her shoulders, like she was intentionally going for some kind of Notorious B.I.G neozootsuit look. The pants, on the other hand, stopped somewhere in that hinterland between ankle and shin.

She was a woman in transition. Below the dangling polyrayon cuffs, she wore scuffed eight hole Doc Martens, one laced green, the other black.

She gestured angrily with a black and yellow *Nightmare Before Christmas* lunchbox.

"Juan, I need that key back! I'm graduating at the end of the semester. The general manager has asked me for it several times."

The lunchbox nearly dinged his top hat.

"And I've asked you for it about a million times!"

Juan flinched, hands reflexively guarding the hat.

"He's writing a recommendation letter for me so that my summer internship at the NPR station turns into a permanent job in the fall."

She quickly turned this into a referendum on the state of the relationship.

"I'm not the only one graduating soon. What's your plan? For us?"

I wouldn't have taken the bait, but Juan did, with flair, stepping forward and fingering the knotted ends of his "belt."

"My plan includes art. It includes living now. In the present. I am not rushing headlong to a desk, office politics, working for the weekend. The desk will always be there, waiting. Why are you in such a hurry to be its slave?"

The last question was rhetorical. He spun on his moccasin's thin leather sole, his belt ends flailing, and marched into the student center, the automatic doors nearly pinching the trailing fringe of his robe.

I followed, adding a hasty, "Hi, I'm David. Nice to meet you," as I walked by Gale. She harrumphed like Miss Piggy.

Juan didn't want to talk about it once I caught up with him, which clued me in to the seriousness of the situation. He generally wanted to talk, at length, about everything. Instead, he focused intently on timing, sound levels, guitar tone, and all the other things he generally categorized "details," as in, "Let me focus on the big picture and you can refine the details." We didn't have much time at all.

• • •

The constant recording sessions took their toll on my already anemic work ethic. A string of opening shifts followed the late nights on campus. As often as possible, I'd squat in the corner of my section on a wooden stool nestled between the Brontës and Conrads and stare at the gray brown carpet, wishing I had some reason to freefall onto its Stainmastered filaments. I'd keep my eyes closed to the count of five with every blink, thinking if I did this enough, I could trick my body into believing it had slept. No one could see me. The Spanish language shelf buffered me from the help desk. Or so I thought. On one morning that stretched interminably towards lunch, I opened my eyes to find Lisa's wrinkled beak inches from my face. Inhaling with surprise, I could smell the noxious Aqua Net that hardened her silver hair like Magic Shell. I tried some tale, a twitchy sty resulting from a misplaced chopstick at the sushi bar, but she wasn't impressed.

"David, don't make me send you home. You don't want to limit your contributions to the store. We rely on you, and," fake smile, "you have so much to give."

As much as I hated Booksalot, I needed the money. I did not aspire to model employeehood, but there were limits to slackishness. Chastened by Lisa's interruption, I surged with productivity. I sprinted to the backroom as soon as Lisa announced the arrival of a book shipment over the intercom. I recommended books to customers. I even volunteered to clean the bathrooms out of a genuine desire to be helpful—or rather appear helpful—and not out of a scurrilous urge to pilfer the copies of *Penthouse* that accumulated in the men's room day after day. I think that's why I picked up the phone when Claire paged "David, line 2" over the intercom. I was in the rare mood to do as I was told.

"David! Hey buddy, glad I got a hold of you. You're hard to get at."

It was Sean. I tried to get off the phone.

"Oh, hey man. I can't really talk here at work . . ."

"Yeah, yeah. You've told me that before. Listen, I just need a quick word with you. I'm sitting on a letter here that I don't want to send. Here, let me read you a bit of it: 'as per Section 3.b of the recording and distribution contract signed and attested to by the undersigned parties, the recipient of this letter has agreed to provide satisfactory evidence of progress towards the fulfillment of all contractual obligations within a timely manner.'"

Unlike their press releases, this, you could tell, had not been drafted in the bong filled office of their warehouse.

"As you can guess, it wasn't me or Mike who wrote that. It was a lawyer friend of ours. Now, if I send this, I'm going to send it certified, so I have a record it's been received. Do you understand what I'm telling you?"

"Yes."

"Good. Now let me ask you something. Do you have any plans to send something to me? Plans to send something soon? I hope you do, because we're putting something together and I need to know if you'll be in on it. You know who Dan Seagrave is, right?"

Of course I did. His paintings looked like what you'd get if H.R. Giger designed an Ewok village. They graced the covers of so many albums that defined death metal: Entombed's *Left Hand Path*, Morbid Angel's *Altars of Madness*, Dismember's *Like An Everflowing Stream*. Moreover, his paintings defined my wardrobe. At least half of my shirts featured some Seagrave necropolis.

"We've contracted him for four pieces. Well, it's actually one piece and we're using it for four covers, one for each death metal album we're releasing this summer. The guy's not cheap these days, even though he'd be drawing Dungeons and Dragons modules otherwise. Anyway, we figured your new album—I'm just assuming you've got something put together—could use one. We're planning an all out promo blitz for you guys, for all our death metal bands. We've got posters of each cover. We're calling it 'The Rising Storm of Death.' Valhalla needs to be in on this."

I hadn't yet told him that Valhalla had imploded, gone on its own Katabasis, but never returned. I tried to explain, but couldn't quite get him to understand that Valhalla no longer existed, that there was just Katabasis, and that the new release, tentatively titled *In Circle of Ouroboros*, had just four songs: "See, the other guy, Juan, and I, we're on a musical katabasis," and here I launched into a completely bardian explanation.

"It's a musical journey into the underworld. The music represents the circle of Ouroboros, a giant, mythical serpent. The songs reflect the churning toll of the serpent's plates against the ocean floor. Conceptually, the listener accompanies us on a katabasis through the music as we encounter the meditative embrace of the Ouroboros."

After the hours spent with Juan, this all seemed perfectly logical to me. But not to Sean.

"Damn, David. You're making things really difficult for me. Here I am trying to get you in on this promo plan with other up and coming bands," he listed their names, all groups I knew and admired, "and you're jerking my chain. Plus, I'm trying to send you guys out on tour this summer. You used to talk about this all the time when *Thrones* came out. Remember. We told you we wanted to do that, but we just didn't have the resources at the time. Now we have more resources, we're commissioning Dan fucking Seagrave paintings, and you can't get me a tape. Remember that letter I read from, man. I don't want to move in that direction, but we will if we have to."

I just said, "I'll mail you something by the end of the

week." Then I headed back to my mop.

After work, I slogged through traffic, anticipating another solitary night with the Paisano jug. I walked up the stairs and heard what sounded like a particularly morose grandfather clock ringing the hour of its demise. Juan sat on my doormat playing this forlorn dirge on a tiny green plastic recorder shaped like a pickle. Or rather, Juan, in a button down oxford shirt and khakis, topped, for good measure, with a ship captain's hat, sat on my doormat playing a pickle.

He dropped the recorder on the ground as soon as he saw me.

He wailed "Gale...she left me!" and burst into racking sobs. A rustling kitchen curtain across the hall caught my eye. The neighbors, mostly senior citizens, moved slowly in the hall, stairway, and, often absurdly so, the laundry room, but they were fleet fingered when it came to the Gables police hotline. One afternoon, a cop pounded on the door after I popped some popcorn.

"One of your neighbors," he'd said, pointing his squawking walkie-talkie at the bowl in my hand, "thought she heard something suspicious."

Who knew if Coral Gables' finest were already en route to investigate this domestic disturbance. To those fools, a pickle looks a lot like a gun. I took Juan's hand and helped him up from the doormat.

"Come on, let's go to the Crown and Garter, man."

I checked my watch.

"We've got half off Guinness pints till 7."

• • •

The bartender plopped down two frothy pints of Guinness. I handed over a five and gestured I didn't need change. Gables rent was a bit higher than other parts of the city, but I considered happy hour at the Crown and Garter an amenity that paid for itself. I took the fullest of the two glasses, handed the other to Juan, then guided us to a table.

Juan thanked me for the beer, took a sip, and exhaled.

"We went to Le Provencal. It's a French restaurant, right up the street here. 'Grownups' go there. Continental cuisine. What could be more mature? I wanted to make amends with Gale. She is not like us. I love her," he teared up a little, "but she's not. She's like a child right now, unquestioningly accepting that the next 'life stage' as she calls it is one that lacks imagination and beauty. I thought making reservations at Le Provencal would show her that even the most mature, serious restaurant one could think of has whimsy at its core. I planned to order escargot. We've had it there before. You get a special fork, more like a trident for toddlers, really, to extract them from the shells. They're submerged in a marinade of basil, garlic, and butter. They're swimming in their self-secreted spiral. We went there on one of our first dates. I was so nervous then. I kept one of the shells, drilled a hole in it, and tied it in my hair. I had it for a year until I lost it while swimming at the beach."

They hadn't reconnected over broiled snails.

"We sat down. We sat outside. This is the best time of the year and this is the one part of the city I enjoy. I hope that when the ocean swallows Miami, it will leave Coral Gables as a tiny islet, a bastion of sun-drenched Spain tickled by the tide. Anyway, we were sitting there, and Gale hadn't said anything about my clothes."

He touched his collar and absent-mindedly unbuttoned one side.

"I said Gale, I can do this, too. See this shirt, these khakis. It's a costume. I know more about costumes than most people. When you wear a costume, you use it to play a part. But it also uses you to get that part played. I told her that I was worried about her, about us. I told her I understood why she was changing the way she dressed. I told her I understood that things cost money, that we live in a capitalist society, and that most people are compelled to fall in line at some point or other. And that's when the snails came, the waiter in a bow tie and cummerbund. Maybe I didn't go far enough? Maybe I should have dressed more formally? In France, they call that a costume—a 'costume,'" he pronounced it so it sounded like "co-tomb."

"I told her that, but maybe she would have been more receptive if I was the one in full formalwear. So the waiter leaves, we're sitting outside, it's a beautiful evening, and we have this aluminum tray between us, this aluminum tray with little indentations. It looks like a palette. In each indentation, a snail. It's $12.99 for eight snails. I said Gale, why do people eat snails? It can't be for their nutritional value. Or that they're particularly filling. A few snails does not a meal make, as I'm sure you can surmise. At one point, they probably ate them because they were poor. In winter or something. That was the only thing to survive. I asked her why people still eat them. Because it's not the obvious thing to eat."

I didn't see where this was going.

"So, you're eating snails at a fancy restaurant, you guys are talking about your feelings, and . . . ?"

"Then I showed her this, the tattoo I told you I'd been planning to get. I finally had it done last week." He undid the middle buttons of his shirt and spread it open with one hand and pointed to it with the index and middle fingers of his right hand, like Jesus gesturing to the sacred heart. The same image he had pasted on the piano room wall now nestled in a coil around his heart, its toothsome jaws poised to snap at the translucent indentation of skin stretched over breastbone.

"The Ouroboros," we said simultaneously. I beamed at my recall, like a student acing a pop quiz. I rewarded myself with a swig. The thorned tips of the skeletal lattice of its wing grazed the brown circle of his left nipple.

"And now it surrounds my heart like it circles the earth. I showed it to her and she, like you, knows what it is, but she wasn't impressed at all."

A loud "Hunh" echoed from the pint glass held to my mouth. Guinness foam nearly cascaded through my nostrils as I choked down laughter and a thick mouthful of stout. What kind of chick would be wowed by some serpent tattoo?

"Instead, she asked me how much it cost!"

"Oh?" The girl impressed me more and more. I wondered the same especially since, Guinness nearly gone, the only thing keeping me from another pint was calculating if Juan's moochiness would invalidate my happy hour discount. He made no move to buy the next round.

"So what'd you tell her?"

"That I'd wanted it for a long time. That in many ways, my tattoo, my inscription of the eternal serpent on my skin, is no different than what she's doing by purchasing new clothes, choosing a new costume to present to the world. What is an action common to all serpents? They slough off their skin, which is replaced anew. The difference is that I am keeping a constant reminder of that transition. I told her that, and told her I thought she was trying to leave the past behind and that it was clear that I belonged to that past. I told her too—by this point we'd scarfed down the escargot and the waiter had brought the bill—that the lowly snail is not that different from the Ouroboros, in that both feed on the past, represented by the serpent's tail and literally by the decaying matter—compost, really—that the snail feeds on as it slimes its way across the forest floor. And the shell, too, is a spiral, an eternal shape, transmuted from that compost. Ancient cultures knew this, knew it to be sacred knowledge. That's why the Romans viewed it as an elite food. To eat an animal is to gain its knowledge. I told her that no matter how elite or high class she wants her life to be, she'll always be moving closer to, not further away from, the things that matter, the things that have been important parts of our relationship. I told her I didn't want her to forget that, to forget me. I told her I am growing, progressing, too, and that she has to respect how I'm doing that."

It sounded like they had as grown up a relationship conversation as you could expect from Juan. More monologue than dialogue. But grownup or grownupish all the same. I didn't see how this led to Juan on my doormat playing a pickle flute.

"That's when the waiter came by to pick up the check. It started to get crowded—I think he needed the table. It was the pre-show crowd for the theater down Miracle Mile. I thought she'd get it—the check. She knows I don't have money for things like that. I barely have enough to get by. My parents came here from Cuba with nothing. My mother doesn't work. She barely even leaves the house."

"Ooh." The last remnant of foam clung to the bottom of the glass like tub sealant. It was quarter to seven, when 2 for 1 ends. Although I was about to buy him another beer, I didn't sympathize with the guy.

"I mean, look at me. Do I look like someone who throws his money away? So the waiter's standing there, I'm waiting for Gale to take the bill, and she just stands up and says, 'Juan, today's my birthday. I'm sick of being limited by your immaturity,' and she just left."

I asked him how he got out of the restaurant. By my calculations, he should still be scrubbing snail tins in the back of Le Provencal for at least another hour or so.

"Oh," he answered meekly, "I scoured twenty dollars—half of it change, quarters and dimes, mind you—out of the corners and crevices of my bag. That's where I found the ocarina, too," he said, now grinning and holding up the pickle flute.

9. Ultralimited

I sent the master tapes, the lyrics, liner notes, everything. Even the Ouroboros painting Juan insisted we use as cover art, despite the Dan Seagrave retrospective I culled from my record collection and closet. We couldn't turn back. We had no choice. Gale got the key from Juan not long after his failed French dinner. When he told me, a hickey the size and color of a ripe plum incarnadined the side of his neck. It was not an even trade.

Once I sent the package, I braced myself for the next call from Sean. I resolved to just answer the phone, get it over with. I couldn't avoid them forever. I sharpied the word "demo" on the master tapes, but I didn't think we'd get the chance to re-record *In Circle of Ouroboros*. If they hated it, I planned to ask Abel if he could help me out. His friends supposedly had a studio in a warehouse out in Kendall. Plus, he managed to start dating Claire, so I figured I could persuade him somehow that I'd cajoled her into going out with him and that he owed me.

Sometimes I thought I hated *In Circle of Ouroboros*. Was it "satisfactory" as per my contractual agreement? I wondered. It did not rock. Percussion was sparse: we'd managed one surreptitious kettledrum rustling, pushing a drum loaded cart with speed and deliberation across the empty parking lot separating the music building from the student center on a moonless night and then back again as dawn slashed the horizon. Juan's obsessions suffused the main songs, "In Circle of Ouroboros," "The Song of Amergin," and "Kithairon." Two sample-heavy instrumentals, "Microcosmos I" and "Micro-cosmos II," melded aimless distortion with magnified insect chatter we sampled from some nature documentary. The whole thing sounded more Dead Can Dance than "Dead by Dawn."

So when the phone rang that afternoon, I picked it up expecting the worst. Sean, though, seemed in good spirits.

"What's up, David? I listened to the new material. I have a proposal for you. Here's what we want to do. We're starting a new series, 'Ultralimited Underground,' and we think this should be the first one we put out."

"Ultralimited?"

"Yeah. A lot of collectors buy our stuff, tape traders, you know? They love limited releases. A thousand copies. Numbered, like your demo tape, but pressed on a CD and distributed to all the core shops. Like Yesterday and Today."

It sounded pretty good. Ultralimited. It sounded exclusive. Underground. It sounded like they wanted to reward us for branching out, for moving beyond that Florida death metal template. Underground. Hard to believe, but they liked it.

"And you think that's okay—that's better than the other thing you talked about? The Dan Seagrave cover?"

"Oh . . . the 'Rising Storm of Death'?"

"Yeah."

"Oh definitely. I mean, what you've got here is really going to help us, and you, too, of course. I mean, think about it, right? This music's getting more popular. I just heard that Morbid Angel signed with a major—but real music is about the underground, about that hard to find release that just blows you away because it doesn't sound like anything else. The true fan knows that, and this release—the Kataba circle—"

"*In Circle of Ouroboros.*"

"Right. It's going to appeal to that true fan. Besides, now it's like lame kids at the mall'll be wearing Morbid Angel shirts. You don't want that."

"Yeah." It did sound ridiculous. "Or you'll hear 'Chapel of Ghouls' on the radio."

"Exactly. That would suck. They just want to always take the true stuff. Commodify it. But that's not going to happen here. Plutonic Records is the real deal. We stand by you guys, the underground."

I couldn't believe they actually liked it. A thousand copies wasn't a lot, though.

"Well, here's the beauty of it. For one, sales of *Thrones* are going to spike. We've still got a bunch of copies of those, and I'm sure they'll go. Plus, once the first thousand are gone, we just press another thousand. Maybe get a different cover design from this new guy you're working with, throw on a rehearsal track. Each pressing is collectible."

"So, it's okay if we don't use the Seagrave cover?"

"Definitely. Like I said, that's one promo we're doing, but this Ultralimited Underground series is something we've been planning, too. We just thought that this release would be . . . uh, different . . . so we didn't mention it to you before. And there's a new band we just signed that we can hook up with the Seagrave cover. This feels right, David. We're excited about how this is all working out."

I stood on my balcony. The air conditioner hummed into action. I pressed the phone tightly to my ear. The earliest touch of summer heat pressed a bit heavier on each afternoon. Where would I be this summer? Here? Rubbing Lotrimin on my balls?

"What about the tour, the European tour you said we'd do to promote the album?"

"I'm going to have to check on that part, David. I'll have to ask Mike. Technically, the money we'd provide for a tour is to promote an album, an LP. But what you've got is more like an EP, so. . . ."

"I don't get it. What we sent you is like 40 minutes long. It is a full length album."

"It is, it is. But it's just three songs . . . three real songs, and then those 'instrumentals.' Are those supposed to be bugs or something?"

"Why does that matter, how many songs it has? I mean, we're not the Beach Boys. We don't need a hit single."

"David, I understand how you feel, but there's a lot more to this than just how long it is. You should be happy we'll release it at all. I mean, I didn't say this earlier, but this isn't really Valhalla. This isn't the band we signed."

"You don't like it?"

"No. No, I didn't say that. I do. I think it's interesting. It's great to smoke to. Good background music. If we didn't like it, we wouldn't release it, would we?" I heard a jangling of glass over the line.

"Hey, Mike just showed up with lunch. Let me talk it over with him and I'll get back to you."

• • •

He never called me back. A few weeks later, the finished product appeared in an envelope tucked under my doormat. I opened the package and sorted through promo copies and tour information. The new album came in a black slipcase emblazoned with an image of Juan's painting that had been reimagined by a graphic artist so that the serpent looked as though it had been forged in bronze and uncovered in some centuries-forgotten hoard. The word "Valhalla," rendered in gold, hovered above the serpent. Below the forged spines that ran the length of the serpent's back, runish script read "Katabasis: In Circle of Ouroboros."

The press release described this as a new Valhalla album, a product of our overbrimming productivity:

Valhalla's second release, "Katabasis: In Circle of Ouroboros," represents a musical journey that begins in the deepest crevices of the mesobenthic depths and ends on the shrouded steepes of vast mountains of madness. This journey is not for the weak or narrow minded.

Only original Valhalla guitarist David Fosberg, adopting the sobriquet "Azrael," and a fellow traveler known only as "The Bard" were up to the task, undertaking this quest and bringing back the slab of molten steel you now hold. Which is why Plutonic Records is offering it as the inaugural release of our Ultralimited Underground series.

The package also contained information on our tour dates and a check. Ten shows over fourteen days. They weren't the cities I expected. Trondheim, not Oslo. Kreutzfeldt, not Berlin. Our tour circled Europe, beginning in Trondheim, heading as far east as Prague, then ending in Antwerp, Belgium. I found a check, for about half the amount we'd agreed on, paperclipped to a note that read "Good luck! This is the best we can do."

I flipped through the itinerary: names of clubs, contacts, dates, even phone numbers of Plutonic reps scattered across the European countryside. At the top of each page, a sternly worded reminder to buy power adapters for our instruments before we left the States. In three weeks, I should find myself far from Booksalot and stepping on stage in Scandinavia. I kept flipping back to the check. Such a low number. Equal to a month or so of full time Booksaloting. With overtime. My stable but unrewarding job for a few weeks of freedom and adventure. Was it worth the trade?

Of course it was. I needed this chance. I bought two tickets, subsidizing Juan. I even bought the right adapters for our instruments and, anticipating Juan strolling through customs, convinced him to pry the razor blades off his "axe." I caught Sean off guard and persuaded him to kick down some more cash. He agreed and, before hanging up, added, "I'll send a stack of shirts and a box of CDs, too. Sell them on tour."

My sister and her husband helped me move out of my apartment. I stored my stuff in one of the many bedrooms in their cavernous suburban villa. I stacked shoe boxes and milk crates crammed with my meager belongings into the closet of a room painted, like every other room, pink (though my sister insisted on calling it "bisque"). I could hear her husband, downstairs, pointing out the obvious:

"Why are we even doing this? He's just going to be gone for a couple weeks."

"He's my brother. My parents say they know he's an idiot, but we have to help him. He's family. That's just how it goes."

"Fine. Just so you know, it's not my fault when he ends up living here. In what's supposed to be—what's going to be—our baby's room."

I never officially quit the bookstore. Instead, I called in sick the morning of our flight. Everyone at the store knew about the tour, except Lisa, which was fine with me because I insulted her precious store in the liner notes. I gave Abel a copy of the album. As my Booksalot career drew to its close, I gloated about the tour whenever I hit him up for coffee. That last week in Miami, he invited me to some show or happening or whatever at the warehouse where his band practiced.

I brought Juan along. But as soon as we stepped into the warehouse, I knew I'd made a mistake. I had become too familiar with his costumes, acclimated to them except on the occasion that he allowed them to influence his behavior, like the time he started singing troubadour songs in the cereal aisle at Publix. Tonight, in khaki leggings and a brown, thigh length tunic, Juan looked like a fortune teller from Tattoine. To top it off, he'd brought his ocarina, which he started tooting on as soon as we got out of the car. Walking next to him, I felt on display, certain that every hipster dude, every sullen chick, regarded us as a pairing even lamer than Riki Rachtman out on the town with Walter Mercado as his wingman.

And that's when I saw her. Natasha. Long, delicate fingers twirling her straight black hair. A brown cardigan pulled tight over the graceful curve of her hip. I hadn't seen her in several months. I felt the same ache of regret, but worse. I stood at the epicenter of regret, powerless, as a stubbly guy in a leather jacket regaled her and a few other girls with some winsome tale of indie rock antics. She pushed a strand of hair over her ear. Even across the room, I could make out the earring, a pewter pentacle, I'd given her so long ago. This guy reached out, took her hand, and kissed it. The group erupted in laughter. She blushed.

I thought of what I'd told Juan, that I cheated on her because she was doing nothing, going nowhere, that I wanted someone with plans, ambitions. Maybe I cheated on her because *I* was doing nothing, going nowhere? We were always the perfect couple, after all.

If she looked over, her eye drawn by a Latino Jedi, her ear by the warbling of his magic pickle, what else would she see? Me. A long haired dirtbag. Then what would I do? The last time I tried to talk to her, she responded with a primal scream and a fist to the eye. I peeled away from Juan, and mumbled something about finding a drink. I hunched my shoulders, and ducked behind a black curtain stretching across the back of the warehouse.

The curtain divided the open display area from a series of rooms in the back. On my side of the curtain, a narrow hallway led to a pair of doors. I guessed one of the doors led to Abel's recording studio. I thought he'd said some bands were playing, but that didn't seem to be the case. Instead, we'd come to some kind of art show, which explained Natasha's presence. A series of geometric murals and poster-size photos of power generating stations hung from the walls. Between the various circles of people talking, sculptures the form and consistency of soggy upholstery rose from the floor. Two of Natasha's paintings—multicolored, Fauvist renditions of the ficus trees at Merrie Christmas Park—hung directly behind the guy who'd kissed her hand. He kept his hand on her at all times. This, I realized, was my replacement. After awhile, they broke away from the group and headed towards the front door. She glided across the room on red patent leather Mary Janes. The dye-soaked edges of her batik print Indian skirt barely brushed the floor. Standing there, hidden, my hands on the curtain, I thought how thick and coarse it felt compared to that skirt. I knew it well, so thin and silky, the feel of it on the back of my hand on the many nights spent necking on the couch in her parents' living room, my palm honing in on her inner thigh. I bet that guy, his hand now on the small of her back as he led her out the door, had similar plans in mind.

Somewhere beneath the Pixies song playing on the PA, I heard my name, and snapped out of my reverie. Abel and his friend, a short guy with a bleached crew cut and diamond studs in each ear, settled just a few feet away from me. I was behind the curtain, though, so Abel didn't see me there. They sipped beers from plastic Dixie cups and trash talked pretty much everyone in attendance. It didn't take long for Abel to bring up my name.

"That guy David's here. You remember that thing I played for you? 'No one knows...what the shadow knows...'?" They broke into laughter.

Just then, Juan walked by. Abel extended his hand, and reeled him in.

"Hey, what's up, man? I'm Abel. I've seen you at Booksalot. I've listened to your album, too."

"Is this the guy?" his friend asked.

"No, this is not David. I mean, Azraelington Maximus," then he grunted, "lord...of...the...night," his lips funneled into a pink windtunnel. "This is Juan." He gestured at the tunic, "You've got, like, your own thing going on. I like it man, I like it. Like this thing. The guy's got a flute necklace or something. Can I try it?" he reached over and lifted the ocarina to his lips. He leaned in close to Juan, the leather strap pulled tight against the collar of his tunic. A thin, reedy tone fluttered in the air.

Juan didn't step away, like I would have.

"This? It's an ocarina, one of the oldest musical instruments on earth. The Mayans and Aztecs played on bird shaped instruments made from clay. The sound represents hope. It's the sound of transcendence beyond gravity, the weight of life."

"Whoa. This thing's on your album, isn't it?"

"Yes, we put so many things in there that represent mythic realms. Even this—it has its significance. For the ancient Mesoamericans, the gods invented not just music, but language as well, from observing cranes and herons. The instrument represents that. And here in this shithole, this ghetto labyrinth, we've consigned those same birds to polluted canals we've dredged to make land for sprawl."

"Heavy, man. That's heavy."

Then he asked Juan, "You don't seem like you listen to metal. You don't, do you? Not like David." His friend lightly punched his shoulder, "Sorry, Tim. I mean, not like Azrael," the grunts again, "lord . . . of . . . the . . . night."

Juan didn't defend me. Instead, he waited for them to finish laughing and said, "It's okay. He's trying to get me into it—he's got me on a mixtape regimen—but I don't know how successful that'll be. Frankly, I'd often prefer listening to Kate Bush, or Siouxsie's *The Scream*."

Abel put his arm around Juan's shoulders.

"I could kiss you, man. You are the coolest motherfucker ever."

Juan continued, "I have my own plans, that's for sure. This is, by no means, my lifework."

Part Two

Is not lead a metal heavy, dull and slow?
   —Shakespeare, *Love's Labour's Lost* (3.1.50)

Angels have no pity
Their wings have turned to stone
   —Cathedral, "A Funeral Request (Ethereal Architect)"

10. Metametal: Ouroboric Liner Notes

Valhalla
Katabasis: In Circle of Ouroboros

Bard: rhythm guitars, ocarina, timpani, transcendence
Azrael: lead guitars, samples, programming, despair

Kithairon

Lyrics: Bard
Music: Bard/Azrael

When the full moon
Rides over us
Listen, listen to us
Sing to you
Kithairon

The god of the high peaks
The wild dervish
On the high peaks

He runs
Kithairon

Where the wind
Is the only thing
That moves
Kithairon
You are the abyss
The breath of the abyss

Microcosmos I
Lyrics: Lucanos elephus
Music: Magicicada/Dracottetix monstrosus

The Song of Amergin
Lyrics: Bard
Music: Bard/Azrael

I am seven battalions
I am a flood on a plain
I am a wind on the sea
I am a ray of the sun

I am the hawk on a cliff
I am gods in the power...
The power of transformation

I am the roaring of the sea
I am a wave of the sea
Who but I knows the secrets of the sea?

Microcosmos II
Lyrics: Nicrophorus tomentosus
Music: Magicicada/ Dracottetix monstrosus

In Circle of Ouroboros
Lyrics and Music: Bard/ Azrael

In circle of Ouroboros
The serpent shrugs beneath the waves
Its burden holds it there
Ouroboros
Jormungandr
Quetzalcoatl

A coral castle is your crown,
The fish are your mantle.
Deathless, one is the all.

The Bard sends blessings to the following:

Robert Graves for constructing such a profound labyrinth as The White Goddess. Consider this our hymn to Her. All insects that contributed their exoskeletal clatter to Microcosmos I and Microcosmos II. H.P. Lovecraft (Ea!), Siouxsie and the Banshees, Joseph Campbell, Jorge Luis Borges, Kate Bush, Italo Calvino, Dead Can Dance, The Cure, Morrissey, Gabriel Garcia Marquez, Type O Negative, Peter Murphy, The Cult, Fields of the Nephilim, Cocteau Twins, Slowdive.

A special dedication to Gale. May you find your true path...?

Complete disregard and apathy to: all simpleminded followers. Your ignorance is your prison.

Azrael would like to thank:

Juan for our collaboration (Death metal renewed!). The Booksalot corporation for giving me this hatred that drives me . . . and for all the free coffee. Hurricane Andrew for destroying everything I thought was permanent. My family for not believing in me. Sean and Mike of Plutonic Records for the motivation to get it done (Euro tour!). Paul Zimmerman and Yesterday and Today Records. All* zines and tapetraders worldwide: you are the underground. Crown and Garter pub (Another Guinness, please!). Merrie Christmas Park for the sylvan paradise in the midst of hell. Everyone who bought Thrones: Hope you like the new one—listen with open ears.

*Except Martin at Cardiac Arrest. I hope Kinko's revokes your copy card. And some guy called Nekrokor: May you lick deez nutz. So shall it be. Your curse did the reverse!

The following bands for influence and inspiration: Candlemass, Cathedral, Solitude Aeternus, Winter,

Malevolent Creation, Death, Cynic, Resurrection, Deicide, Tiamat, Amorphis, Incantation, Demonomacy, Carcass, Napalm Death, Bolt Thrower, Unleashed, Disincarnate, Morbid Angel, Assuck, Obituary, Sepultura, My Dying Bride, Anathema, Thergothon (spiritual brothers!), Disembowelment, and all bands on the Plutonic roster.

11. Trondheim Rock City

The thick brine of pickled herring suffuses the air in Trondheim. You sense, even in summer, that the city lies at the northern rim of human habitation. Sure, postcards in the train station abound for some place called Nordkapp even farther north, but the ten hour trek beyond Trondheim seems needless, unless you suffer from some deep-seated puffin fetish. Trondheim is a tidy Lego village placed at the point where a desolate, lichen covered moonscape meets a desolate, leaden sea. Looking out at the city from the train station entryway, I began to realize I should have consulted a map before agreeing to Sean's tour itinerary. What other forgotten corners of Europe had he booked? It is common knowledge Scandinavians love metal in the same way that Jerseyites love Bruce Springsteen, but, barring a convention of hard-rockin' mycologists, this town did not seem capable of yielding a decent sized crowd for the inaugural performance of the truly underground Valhalla "Katabasis" tour.

The venue, a red domed octagonal building owned by the local university, served as our home base. Besides the club, it housed a hostel, a bar, and a community educational center complete with a kindergarten. A small hand-lettered sign reading "Cathabasic—tonite!" stuck to the door of the bar. We checked in with the bartender, who played a number of other roles, including club promoter, innkeeper, and educational director. He saw Juan, dressed today like some kind of gypsy-sailor, and clapped his hands, saying, "Ha ha! I am loving this. You will perform tonight in this leprechaun costume?" That should have been the first warning sign, but we didn't notice it. Instead, he inundated us with information about food specials at the bar (nothing we could afford for dinner; some kind of spreadable salami in a toothpaste tube for breakfast), our need to rent sleepsacks for the night (ten bucks each for a thin and abrasive body condom fashioned from truckstop papertowels), the amount of money we'd get from tickets sold that night (very small, given the fact that Plutonic sent no posters or flyers, but not to worry, because people love all things Celt-y here in the far north), just about everything except a rundown on the classes held at the center that week. By the time he asked us if we needed help with our bagpipes, we were half way down a hall smattered with construction paper finger paintings and on the lookout for our dorm-style bunk bed.

In those early hours of the tour, we were optimistic enough to think that things would sort themselves out. Sure, the promoter mistook us for a folk act, but so what? People would turn out for the show. Trondheim's small, but it has a university. We imagined that, despite the hundreds of miles separating us from the nearest population center, the slow trickle of people on the nearby high street would coalesce into a crowd of rabid Katabasis fans come nightfall.

As I set up CDs and t-shirts on a table next to the stage, the club owner came in to check on us. Drawn by the golden image of the Ouroboros, he picked up a CD and pointed at the cover:

"This is surely the famous Loch Ness monster, no?"

That's when I started to worry.

• • •

When Valhalla played, the party started well before the show. You'd walk on stage and hear death grunts coming from all directions. The pit sounded like a pond full of bullfrogs clamoring to spawn. Once, in Melbourne, the crowd erupted into a circle pit while I stood on stage, alone, tuning an E-string. When you started playing, you could overcome any nervousness by mindlessly following the random bodies spinning across the pit. You felt calm and in control, like a cat perched in front of a fishbowl. Our Katabasis debut reminded me more of the night Natasha dragged me to a sitar concert on South Beach, a silent room of well mannered raga enthusiasts waiting for one man to align a thousand chakras. How could he handle the pressure?

I strapped on my guitar, and no one moved. At least Ali Akbar Khan could tell himself his motionless, probably napping, fans were only meditating. I didn't know what to think. I walked to the front of the stage and peered out. No bodies pressed against my shoes. No uplifted hands strained to touch my guitar. The pit was exactly that—an empty hole devoid of life. The room wasn't completely empty, though. I could make out the distant silhouette of bodies against the back of the room. A number of still, silent, unresponsive bodies. Did Juan think this was normal? Par for the course at a Kate Bush show, no doubt. Instead of playing, I had to fight the urge to put the guitar down, walk off stage, head to my hostel bunk, and shroud myself in a sandpapery sleepsack.

I stepped to the mic and harangued the audience with an aggrieved death grunt: "Ghooohhh!"

No response.

"Are you dead? Come on, Trondheim!"

Juan strummed the opening arpeggio of "Kithairon," our peppiest number at 55 bpm, and I growled, "This next one's about the fate you can't escape. Kithairon."

It was the longest ten minutes of my life. I'd never had stage fright, imagined I'd only feel it in some impossible future where Valhalla, with Slayer as support, played for raging stadium audiences, but the complete lack of sound, of motion, of energy coming from the crowd nearly stilled my fingers, silenced my voice. My fingers hung from my hand like dead mice on a square of fly paper.

When we got to the last two lines of the song, "You are the abyss, the very breath of the abyss," I felt like I was addressing this terrible audience, and not the magic mountain of classical tragedy. You are the abyss, and there's nothing mystical or revelatory about staring at you. You are the abyss, and I bet you're not planning on buying a t-shirt.

I traced a path along the edge of the stage towards Juan, and eventually dared another glance at the crowd. A few more had streamed in. The abyss wasn't completely empty. As the song died out, I moved to the sampler we'd set up on a small table at the center of the stage. I wanted to keep the sound going so we didn't have to endure complete silence between songs. I cued up our cicada samples and coaxed fuzzy distortion from my guitar as Juan whetted his lips on his ocarina. He played a simplified version of the main riff in "The Song of Amergin."

I eased into the riff too, slowly strumming the guitar. Sharing Juan's mic, I sang the opening lines as he ocarinaed: "I am seven battalions/ I am a flood on a plane/ I am a wind on the sea." And then Juan saved the show. He became less Bon Joker and more Bon Jovi as he fluted away on his plastic pickle. He gestured towards the crowd with one hand, stepped away from the mic, and hung his toes off the edge of the stage. A slight movement rippled through the crowd. Somehow, Juan snake charmed a contingent of swaying goths away from the wall and towards the stage. A row of dudes stayed glued to the back wall, but in Trondheim at least, the bulk (pun intended) of our fan base consisted of Stevie Nickses dipped in ink, forcedfed donuts, and then replicated endlessly in laced bustiers, Ladyhawke gowns with fluted bellshaped sleeves, and velvety, cleavage-baring Snuggies.

He thrust his chest out and reeled them in. He channeled Kenny G, extending the end of the riff into an epic single-note ocarina solo. He peeled his shirt open to expose his tattoo Ouroboros. Juan's show of stage charisma spurred me on. As far as I knew, he'd never performed live, although I suppose his constant costume parade constituted an unending series of performances. Really, he was probably as seasoned as some crusty Las Vegas fixture, some Cher or Barry Manilow. Later, he would tell me it was the White Goddess herself who saved the show, that it was the Celtic source material for the lyrics that made him turn his ocarina solo into a pied pipering of reclusive Norwegians.

"I felt like we were battling the anti-song of Amergin, like someone had cast a spell, a curse, at the stage, erected a magical boundary that kept the audience away. I wanted to bring them to the stage, show them it was safe. I felt like I had to exhale, breathe out that last little bit of Gale holding me back. That one last little piece of predictable, pragmatic reality, suffocating me."

After the show, flanked by two of these fleshy, gothy ladies and wedged in the booth of a bar furnished like an IKEA-fashioned ski chalet, he told me, "I saw all these beautiful women out there and I thought 'These are my people.' They'd appreciate what Gale hadn't. I gave her every chance to be that goddess, but she left me. Maybe she had to so that I could be here?"

By 'here,' he meant cradled between Delphine and Olienna. I was cradled too. There was plenty of room for cradling. Delphine's cleavage burst from her low-cut velvet dress like the twin eggs of some prehistoric flightless bird. Olienna shared the Venus of Willendorf's physique, but carried herself like a beach volleyball pro on defense. She could have bench pressed Juan and me. Simultaneously.

As Juan talked about our fortuitious rally—the show was far from sold out, but we did it, hucked a few discs, and now sat in a bar, with girls—Olienna engulfed her beer like Thor swallowing the ocean. The girls praised us, doted on us as though we were small children. Delphine put her arm around Juan and said, "It was a small crowd, but that's typical for Trondheim."

Olienna rubbed my arm and added, "Especially in the summer. Many students leave for holiday."

"The people there, though. Many important people. I saw Anneke. She writes 'Night Shadows.' It's a local music magazine."

"Some people from Oslo, too. From record labels."

"I don't want to talk about that."

She, too, whipped back the beer.

Olienna went on, "I also saw Eric and Mathias. They play in Dragondance."

Delphine put down her now-empty glass.

"Olienna, you whore. She knows them quite well."

Olienna responded with a cavernous belch.

"The beer . . . it makes me burp!"

Delphine, unfazed, leaned across the table, the exposed domes of her breasts an inch below Juan's nose, and pretended to peer into Olienna's empty glass.

"All gone. Now we show you how we stay warm in the north." She signaled the bartender, and within minutes, a clear bottle and four shot glasses showed up at the table.

Olienna grinned, pulled me between her pendulous breasts, and kissed me long and hard.

I didn't resist.

• • •

The liquor replaced desire with sweet spinning sickness, poisoning Satan's serpent. The next morning found me stretched out on a bath towel on a tile floor. Alone.

My toes bumped against a refrigerator door. I had slept in the kitchen.

I smiled at my good fortune. If I slept alone, on the kitchen floor, then I couldn't have done anything stupid or shameful, right?

Or at least I tried to smile. More of a tortured grimace, really, as I searched for the bathroom. Acrid saliva streamed into my dry mouth. Circling through the apartment, slightly off balance, I stumbled into a tiny toilet closet.

After several vomits, each heave as loud as Olienna's beer

burps, I rested my head on the toilet seat.

A key detail pushed through my thick, cotton hangover: I slept alone, true. I slept alone naked. Why did I sleep alone naked?

And that's when, squatting by the toilet, trying to resolve this paradox, my head between my knees, I noticed the soggy condom strapped to my dick.

In a panic, I raced up the stairs. I remembered snippets of last night—the Norwegian moonshine, followed by techno dancing, then tequila, a boozy walk through Trondheim's empty streets, the exhausted collapse—but nothing shed light on my naked condom-wearing. We must be in the trolls' lair, I thought. That much was obvious. But at what cost? At the top of the stairs, I cautiously peered into an open doorway.

A huge bed sprawled in the middle of a room beshrouded with black velvet curtains and Bauhaus and Depeche Mode posters. I couldn't remember these posters. Or could I? The two women, clearly the goths from last night, slept on either edge of the bed. Their massive brontosaurus thighs tented the sheets into a green satin mountainscape.

To my horror, Juan's naked brown body, morning wooded, lay between them like a single-masted Viking ship dwarfed by the steep cliffs of a fjord.

12. Don't Break the Oath

After seeing Juan, I just had to get out of the house. The she-trolls lived in a townhouse on a residential street. I vaguely recalled the way back to town, and I hoped to find a coffee shop or something along the way. The hangover carved my mind into a black impenetrable cavern. I couldn't—or wouldn't—access my memories from last night. Did I—did Juan—hook up with these chicks? Simultaneously? Had we, so to speak, "crossed swords"? I shuddered. What would Natasha think if she could see me now, depraved and debauched? I had slaked my thirst with the waters of Nepenthe, only they never told you its waters were bottled as Norwegian moonshine.

The sun warmed my skin and comforted my ravaged body. The suburban sidewalk gradually gave way to a meandering fitness trail following the shore of a different kind of mythical river, a pleasant grass shored stream. Occasionally, I stopped to puke onto a bush. As I walked, I could tell I was, in fact, getting closer to town, though I didn't recognize landmarks from last night. These memories, too, had been drowned in a fleshy fjord. But the buildings along the path stood closer together, and rows of parked cars separated this linear park from the street. Ahead, a brick bridge, its top marked with turrets, arched over the path. I walked underneath it and found myself on what I can only describe as a Norwegian beach. There was no ocean, just the

93

lazy stream I'd been following that, at this point, had dwindled to a thread of water about the width of the bike path I walked along. There was no sand, either. Instead, a grassy hill sloped upwards to meet the bridge.

I knew it was a beach because of the topless girls. It was not a "topless beach," a phrase suggestive of a nasty place, some forlorn strand where balding men slather sun ripened wieners with Solarcaine, in the same way that Miami Beach is not a "topless beach" even though there are topless girls as far as the eye can see. It was a beach in a place where it's socially acceptable for girls to cavort in breathtaking toplessness, their pert titties flush from the breeze.

I didn't notice at first. No one else seemed to; there weren't parents pointing in disgust, then shielding their children's eyes. People sat on the hill sipping coffee, talking, minding the groups of children playing. Head heavy with hangover, I was overcome by the urge to lie on the hill, absorb the sun, and allow it to absorb the black cloud of my blackout.

I looked for a convenient spot: not directly downhill from the trio of tumbling kids, not downwind from the elderly pipe smoker—the tobacco smell would definitely disgorge a gallon of chum, not too close to the guy in a suit reading the newspaper. As I stood there, my synapses firing mostly blanks, two girls—one twiggy brunette, another with a bleach blonde pageboy and chunky glasses—stopped a few feet away. They put down their bags—enormous purses each about half the size of my hiking pack—and a plastic bag with snacks and bottled water, stripped off their shirts, unclasped their bras, and sprawled their bare-chested bodies on the grass.

I found myself on the grass in moments, any thoughts of locating a more perfect spot abandoned. The brunette had skin as brown as a newly stained deck, her lithe body untainted by anything approximating a tan line. A layer of light blonde peach fuzz covered her legs and disappeared where her shorts made a half-hearted attempt to conceal her thighs. I started to feel better. Why did no one recommend arousal as a hangover cure?

Her friend did not produce the same ameliorating effect. Her body, an opaque blob of mozzarella, had few curves to distinguish breasts from belly. Juan's kind of woman, I thought, then paused, remembering brief shadowy moments of rough handling (womanhandling?) on the stairway landing in the goths' townhouse.

My kind, now, too?

My thoughts alternated between admiring the view, loathing myself for what may or may not have transpired the previous night, cringing at the very clear memory of our lame show, and enduring long moments of hungover blankness.

After one of those moments, I noticed that some guy had joined the girls. He was short and thin with slightly curly shoulder length black hair. He wore a leather jacket festooned with patches, chains, zippers, and spikes, even though I, spawn of the Caribbean sun, felt like a toasted Pop Tart in the tingly heat of the Norwegian summer and, out of a display of unity with the topless girls, had already stripped off my shirt, kicked off my shoes, and splayed out my socks like garden gnome beach towels. All his fearsome jangly ornaments looked like merit badges in some perverse Scouting troop: Venom appreciation, mystical symbol recognition, advanced knots: focus on chains.

If I'd known better I'd have pegged him as a Katabasis fan, but one thing I hadn't forgotten about last night was what I'd hoped to scour from my mind in the first place, namely the largely empty expanse in front of us as we played, a desolate anoxic region, like the dead zone in the Gulf of Mexico, where an audience should be.

The thin, tan girl bent over her towel and pulled on her top. The larger girl started sorting things in her bag. The heavy metal guy looked over at me and smiled. It looked like they were leaving. I could only imagine what this guy's day planner looked like: barely legal humping at 3, followed by a leisurely stroll to the next gig. I wanted what he had. The

Eurometal lifestyle. It seemed so easy. All he had to do was glide through immaculate manicured cities of medieval towers, planned gardens, and topless beauties by day and then, by night, attend gigs in bars devoted exclusively to metal minstrelsy. He'd do this for the rest of his days, long after I'm gone, re-yoked in the service of a service economy.

Lost in my jealous reverie, I didn't notice that the girl I had been staring at now stood over me. I squinted, blocked the sun with my hand, and said hello.

"Bård," she gestured over her shoulder to the guy, who nodded at me, "wants that you should come with us."

Why not? I thought. Hungover or not, I deserved at least one Eurometal afternoon in my life.

• • •

We sat in a booth of a bar painted a garish deep purple. Bright yellow carvings of the man in the moon, exactly like the amulet one of the Bon Jovi dudes wore in their *Slippery When Wet* period, or the Proctor & Gamble logo, peered from the corners and hung from the walls. Bursts of yellow, orange, and white paint streamed across the purple ceiling, creating a chaotic universe of cascading comets and blazing novas. Two Carlsberg steins and a platter of cheese cubes skewered with multicolored toothpicks sat between us.

"So . . . you are here in Norway for the Metallica concert, surely?"

This guy, Bård, the Nordic version of Bart, sneered at me over the top of his beer. His eyes were as black and inky as the LaBrea tar pits in their sabertooth swallowing heyday. He seemed vaguely threatening and, jacket removed, a little smelly, too. Tufts of black armpit hair poked out from his cut off black t-shirt. Charred burns the size of cockroaches pebbled his arms. Clothed and unexposed, the girls seemed a bit younger than I'd thought at first. Thalia and Grete, the hot girl and the fat friend, peeled away from us as soon as we walked in the bar. They joined a packed table of raucous high schoolers. What could they see in him?

"Huh. Metallica?" I wasn't sure if this was a test, a joke, or some kind of veiled insult. Sure, everyone likes Metallica, but you can tell a lot about a Hessian by his level of devotion to the band. In a pop context, I guess it would be like asking someone what their favorite Beatles song is. The occasional easy listener might cite "Love Me Do" while the true collector would argue for some obscure rarity from the *Revolver* sessions. His jacket hung across the smooth polyester back of the booth—also purple—and I could see a Mercyful Fate patch, a Venom patch, a Bathory pewter pin in the shape of a goat's head, but nothing alluding to Metallica fandom, no M and A lightning bolted into the archetypal heavy metal logo, no field of gravestones with the souls of the dead manipulated by puppet strings, no electric chair carried through the sky on a storm blast.

"What do you mean?" I asked, taking in the opening strains of "Youth Gone Wild" playing through the jukebox. I found myself in, I realized, a rocker bar. These are practically nonexistent in Florida. Even the Button South played progressive favorites, new wave dance grooves, most nights. Maybe he was serious? I hadn't listened to Metallica since tenth grade, when they released the dreaded black album. I wasn't even aware it'd come out until some muscle-car obsessed oboist in the marching band told me he now "understood" where I was coming from since he'd purchased this supposedly life changing album. That was the first strike against it. Second was the report I read in *Spin* of James Hetfield extolling the virtues of his vocal trainer who helped him not to achieve the operatic four octave brilliance of King Diamond or glass pane splintering power of Messiah Marcolin, but simply add a hard-edged patina to Bob Seger's silver bullet shitbag elegies of getting laid in pappy's Oldsmobile. The final strike against the album was the music itself. Gone were the minor key tonalities, the epic explorations of a melody to its harmonic limits. These had been replaced by pop structures and a macho overawareness of the crunchy "power" of a power chord, each one strummed, presumably, with the aim of inciting a touchdown dance. I think that last point, more than anything else, an abbreviated list including the cropped haircuts, the stone washed denim vests replaced by satin baseball jackets like the kind sold to Hard Rock Cafe culinary tourists, the lyrical abandonment of social commentary and occult thematics (what did that leave them to sing about?), led me to abandon Metallica and left me unable to listen to the first four records without wondering, like '80's teenstress Tiffany, what could have been so beautiful, so right. No wonder the entire Southridge Spartans marching woodwinds grooved to it.

"Are you serious?"

"They played last night in Oslo. It was a heavy metal exodus from all corners of the country. The forest trolls of Bergen. The pretentious wankers in the Oslo death metal scene. Even the small town types and university students here in Trondheim. It was a festive reunion, I'm sure."

I wasn't sure what he was telling me. He smirked, daring me to ask the obvious question. Why hadn't he gone, then?

"You're sure? Weren't you there, too? Oslo's like five hours south."

He glanced over at the girls' table.

"I have my own reasons for being here. But you haven't yet answered me. What are you doing here? This is a long way to travel for girls. Of course, from what I hear, they are all fat in America, so there's a possible motive. Although," and now he eyed the short-haired blonde's meaty ass as she stepped to the bar, "that can be fun, too."

"Oh. I'm ... uh. I'm a musician. I'm. ..." I was going to tell him I was on tour, too, but I felt too embarrassed. Did it count as a tour if there was no audience? "A Metallica concert's a big deal here? Some kind of event?"

"And they're not in the US? Have you not heard the black album?" He did a half volume Hetfield: "'*Go to never never land*.'"

"You didn't have to miss it. You could have taken your

ladies with you, like on a date. Or a field trip."

"Well said, well said." He saluted me with his glass. "Now I will tell you the truth. I was also at a concert last night. That is my reason for being here. Have you ever heard of the band Katabasis? Yes, I was at your show last night. I am no Metallica fan, though many are. More out of childhood nostalgia, I'd say, than out of any real interest in their creative path. And, I'll say it lest we awkwardly overlook the obvious, I was one of the few there, the very few."

I felt the urge to defend myself, mustering half words and syllables, "well, uh . . . uh," though, of course, he was right.

He held his hand up to silence me.

"There's no need. I rather prefer that sort of atmosphere. No mosh pit calisthenics, skinheads dashing us all with their doltish sweat. It was a good show. Whoever missed it, that is their loss. Really, I'd say it's the loss of your label. I looked at your tour calendar. Do you know that you will be playing in the same country, sometimes the same city, on the same night as Metallica for every single date of your tour? It's true that they are no longer the metal vanguard, but here in Europe, they are like your Jimmy Buffett. No one wants to miss a good party. And Katabasis is no party."

In just a few days, we'd be in Prague, the first big city on the tour and where I'd thought our luck would change. But now I knew that probably wouldn't be true. If this guy was right, we'd just fizzle out, then return to Florida, defeated and forgotten.

"I have brought you here, I have given you beer. I have told you that I saw your show. Yet I have told you little of myself, besides my name. You may know me by another name, a stage name, a name that will clarify my interest in your music. Have you ever heard of someone called 'Nekrokor'?"

The name took me back to that night in Miami, after John and Phil had made it clear that Valhalla was over. You remember: "I come to bring you death death death." The ashy dust coating the bottom of the envelope. The ripped scraps of black construction paper marked in chalk with impossible letters, Russian, Hebrew, or some obscure Orcish dialect. The threat letter from the guy now sitting across from me. The death threat from the guy who'd bought me a beer. Suddenly, the bar seemed a bit too empty, too remote. Emptier than a Katabasis show, even. The girls had filed out with their friends into the sunshine baking the pub's outdoor terrace. That left about four other people inside. Had he lured me here, intentionally, to finish what he'd promised in his air mailed missive?

"I ... uh ..." I fumbled with my glass, cursing myself for letting him buy the first round and bring it from the bar. In nearly any other setting, the idea of drugged beer wouldn't sound quite so bad, but here ... so far from home, with only incompetent, impractical Juan to initiate a search to save my sorry ass? I looked over to the bar, where a heavily muscled and pierced Hessian type glared at our table while towel drying a rack full of steins. Growing up with my dad's incessant whiskey-fueled provocations, I'd learned early on that you can't out-aggress an unstable aggressor. Best to play it cool, I thought.

"Yeah ... Nekrokor. I think I've heard of you. You're a ... uh ... tape trader, right?"

He laughed. "I expected you to be more forthright. A brash American. I also run a record label. You know that to be true. You should also know that you have touched something important in your Katabasis record. It was not something I thought you capable of accessing. You can relax. Sit back. Finish your drink. You do not have to be afraid—I have revoked my curse. Let me tell you about your music. You should enjoy this—it will be like a fan testimonial, but hopefully not as ludicrous as the promotional materials Plutonic likes to peddle. I remember the first time I heard your album. I opened the promo package from Plutonic—I like to keep myself informed on the competition, compare their steady stream of drivel to the carefully orchestrated line of masterworks I am preparing for release—and saw, initially, the photo of you and your brother in arms, the Spaniard. I felt a pulse of joy. Had my spell succeeded in killing off 80% of a terrible death metal band? Where were the other fools? My magical prowess silenced a torrent of blast beats? I read the promo flyer with interest. The band was and was not in existence. 'Katabasis'—I recognized the allusion. This was the next Valhalla album and was not the next Valhalla album. The other musical prodigies in your group were pursuing their studies. And at an American university. No doubt the depth of those studies was not particularly difficult to imagine. I believe my spell must have worked in some inverted manner. Yes, when you unsealed the letter I sent you, it was to unleash a curse of destruction. I know that you opened the letter. I sensed it. That is how magic works. And yet somehow the curse endowed your music as a vehicle capable of reaching the submerged depths of the secret city of the soul. I can no longer listen to death metal because it is all surface. True, a complex surface of shifting beats and countless riff changes, but a surface nonetheless. In particular, the American variety grew to embrace all the stupidities of your culture. An album like *Altars of Madness* remains timeless, as it gives voice to the nameless voice of the deep, but since then, that music has become empty headed pop for school children. I found your Valhalla album to be the epitome of this idiocy. Imagine my surprise to be sitting here now, with you, a person who I had ritually cursed through international air mail, and on the brink of offering that person a contract on a label that represents only the truest and most exclusive artists."

"You want to sign my band?"

He briefly met my gaze, did something like a grimace, like this was actually quite painful for him, and then continued as though he hadn't heard my question at all.

"It was something I did not expect, something that had never occurred. A move away from the brutal through an inward turn? To be truthful, I am not interested in 'keeping up' on new releases. I only have service from larger American labels so that I can sell the promos to idiots and obsessive collectors. I remember the thrill of joy I felt when I realized that Valhalla had imploded. Oh yes, I could interpret the subtext of the gushing promotional flyer. I realized they had not, as a result of my spell, desisted and died. It was not, as the publicists reported, some explosive expression of creativity on your part, or a simple intermediary release before the next official Valhalla album. I receive packages from Plutonic at least every other week or so; they may have no ear for music, but they certainly have a nose for promotion. And I, of course, read their catalog to make sure that they are stocking Despondent Abyss titles. I had not missed the advertisement declaring Valhalla's triumphant return to form. It was clear that you had been abandoned by your band. I put on *In Circle of Ouroboros* expecting a familiar experience. The first track started like any other Florida death metal album—ominous keyboards, some sound effects evoking chains dragged across an oceanic waste. It would be no more than a minute or so before a formulaic 'Zombie Ritual'-style chorus would result in another CD used to fund the Despondent Abyss discretionary fund. But then it began. You kept the keyboards, drenched them in echo and reverb, and added slow, distorted riffs. You abandoned the constant changes of typical death metal, and instead moved from riff to riff by changing something like one note per minute. The dual vocals, a high pitched Scylla and an ocean engulfing Charybdis, trapped me, transfixed, between my speakers."

Now he looked at me directly.

"Yes, I would like to sign your band. Which leads us to the small issue of a contract and," he reached into the folds of his jacket, "our signatures."

He pulled out a dull gray knife with a blade about as long as a pint glass. The knife had a metal pommel guard filled with spikes made from what looked to be roofing nails. He held the knife so it pointed towards the door.

I pushed back from the table. My chair screeched against

the concrete floor. Miamians, we move quickly when we sense violence. When he said he'd "revoked" his death threat, it's possible he meant something else.

The knife looked like some gruesome medieval ancestor of the blade Rambo used to liberate southeastern Asia. Nekrokor laughed a low, steady drumbeat of sound, then pressed the blade on his palm. I'd come to know that laughter well, the mirthless bass sound of *Homo europeanus*.

"Perhaps I overestimated the degree of change possible in you, although it has been not yet a year since I initially wrote you. No matter. Continual change is an element of all things, living and dead. The true agent of this cosmic dynamism sees death and the flesh as symptoms of a chaos demanding of veneration."

With that, he moved the blade like he was going to slice open his entire palm, but repositioned his hand so the tip of the blade met the tip of his index finger. A slow trickle of blood appeared and he ran his finger around the mouth of his beer glass so it was glazed with a thin crimson layer.

Then he handed the knife to me.

I didn't believe in curses or spells, didn't think that melding beer and blood would bond me to Nekrokor as some kind of record-producing zombie thrall, but I could tell by the gleam in his eye as he drained his glass, then licked the bloody rim, that he did. I stared at the big clunky knife in my hand and considered the real pestilences potentially unleashed by its blade: hepatitis, AIDS, maybe even a nasty cold.

"Will you join our ranks?"

• • •

I didn't take it.

"What does that mean, exactly? You know, what are the terms of our contract?"

He put the knife on the table and smiled. The brown sheen of blood coated his front teeth like chunky Paisano flecks. I hoped I hadn't pissed him off. He might have liked it better if I'd taken the blade and given him a good jab.

"It is no surprise to me that Plutonic intends to discard you. That is their way. They are businessmen. Ineffective businessmen, granted, but businessmen nonetheless. That is their model—" and here he listed a stream of heavily hyped bands that after a single album had simply disappeared, "heavy metal one hit wonders all of them. And yet, an effective way to build a company. See . . . if you only produce 1,000 copies, maybe 10,000 at maximum, of a given title, then you have no real responsibility to the artist once those copies have been sold. The problem with producing music comes at three key points of the sales cycle: creating need, meeting distribution, and maintaining need. The first, at least for underground music fans, requires the least amount of effort, for what is an interest in obscure music other than a hunger for novelty? In most cases, this desire for novelty exists as a small symptom of the banal commerciality of your people, of American popular culture. The drive to acquire that obscure Winter EP, for example, is no different than a sudden need to wear only pleated pants, followed after several fashion cycles by a need to never wear pleated pants. The manifestation of this consumer addiction as an ongoing process of acquiring underground music effects a limited number of easily accessible consumers, which gets us to our second point, meeting distribution. Have you ever wondered why Plutonic, a record label with a roster of its own artists, spends so much time and energy assembling a mail order catalog filled with albums from bands of all labels? You can even buy fairly commercial items, such as live albums by Deep Purple, or, in a particularly humorous business move, a set of early Whitesnake demos.

"They do this to secure their position as a key distributor of goods. To this extent, they capitalize on their dual role as merchant and marketplace. I admire what they have created in that regard, because they have taken an informal system established by true fans scattered across the globe and formalized it. Yes, I have been in contact with Sean and Mike since the early '80's through tape trading. I believe I first contacted Mike because I had heard from a Bulgarian friend that he had a Lucifer's Heritage demo. I sent a sheet of International Reply Coupons from Norway to some small town in the United States so I could get a copy of a tape from a German band. Circuitous and inefficient? Of course. The main advantage of tape trading, however, was to enable the tape traders who became distributors. Some remained fans, consumers, while others transitioned into business owners. Take the most promising demos, reward a small recording budget, press limited runs of LPs and 'ultra rare' EPs, and use the journalistic platform enabled by a cheap Xeroxed zine. These are the simple steps that create a need. Their company, as you are now experiencing, fulfills the other two necessary conditions of the underground music model in innumerable and, shall we say, remunerative ways. Their most direct means of meeting distribution needs are simple enough to understand. You subscribe to their mailing list, they send a catalog, and you purchase from the comfort of your home. By promoting and signing bands, they generate interest and maintain sales. But the hardest part of this cycle is to maintain the need for a specific band, for the product they produce. And here is where you have been. . . ."

"Fucked over," I cut in.

"Yes . . . by the ultralimited mentality. I noticed you selling CDs after your show last night. How many did they give you to sell?"

"A box of about a hundred. Maybe twenty t-shirts, too."

"And here is the main reason you consider a change. I would not be surprised if those are the only copies of your album in existence on this earth. You are on a fool's errand, visiting the areas with only the most dedicated collectors, and once you have completed your own Ouroboros-like circling of the European perimeter, you will have fulfilled your purpose. The Plutonic business model does not intend to maintain need or build the prestige of its artists. Did I mention that these people come from a small American farm town? That is the way of all rural people—they are aggressively shortsighted. Rural Americans? The height of myopia."

"Hey," I protested, but didn't add anything else in their defense. Nekrokor described a system I'd lived and belonged to, but hadn't seen it as that, as a system or business model. I'd seen the constant emergence (and less-considered disappearance) of bands as a mark of a vibrant scene, a sign of constant evolution and shifting borders.

"They will do nothing to help you develop your artistic vision. Ultimately, they are only collectors. Instead, it is in their best interest to move to another band, another sound, and wash their hands of you."

He told me what I knew to be true, but didn't want to admit to myself. The tour had been arranged as a swan song, an errant quest, to sell the ultralimited exclusive copies of our album, primarily arranged to meet the few areas of potential sales, but also designed to discard Katabasis through the rewardless toil of our epic self-financed schlepping across the European continent. They'd provided us with 20 shirts to sell, because that's how many they had made. They'd given us a box of 100 copies of our album because, in all likelihood, that's how many remained. We were not that different from the Ouroboros itself. At each stop of our tour, the serpent swallowed itself further. By the time we got to Amsterdam, the serpent would disappear, swallowed whole. It would simply cease to exist. From the Plutonic point of view, we would expend our energy, and my money, to shill the last of their products. Sean had told me before the tour that because Valhalla wasn't technically a band anymore, Plutonic was under no obligation to fulfill their end of the contract. On the other hand, as Katabasis stood in for Valhalla, we had been under obligation to do the tour.

"So how is what you're offering me any different?"

"I am not actually offering you anything. At a certain point in the past, I moved beyond the role of tape trader, guitar player, record label director. Instead, I have become a mere agent for something much greater. Tell me, about midway through the title track, there's a passage that I have wanted to ask you about. It comes right after you sing the lines 'The serpent shrugs beneath the waves....'"

And here he sang them in a rich, melancholy tenor, making them sound to me, the guy who wrote them, like something from a medieval folk song, or some fragment of a monk's polyphonic chant that had gone terribly awry. The bartender looked up from drying beer glasses and the strains of the Scorpions faded for that moment.

"I want to know how you and your Spaniard felt when you first recorded it."

I knew what he was getting at. It was a response so different than anything you'd expect from Sean or Mike. For them, music was just a surface. If they liked something, they'd say it was 'godly' or it made them shit themselves. If it didn't have a blast beat, it didn't really move them. They always talked about music like it was a laxative in collectible packaging. Nekrokor, though, identified something in the song that moved the soul.

After that line, "The serpent shrugs beneath the waves," you've got about a minute or two of buildup. The bass lumbers from low G for two beats, then to B flat, to D, then back to E sharp. A layer of keyboard effects follow the bass, but the echo and reverb combine, moving the bass from the foreground to the background about midway through the passage. Juan's guitar starts about a half measure off, then slowly aligns itself with the bass, moving into the foreground just as the reverb wave washes it away, then, all instruments in unison, the bass amplified and deepened, so it's now like the slow thud of a drowned timpani picked up on radar, the second line, "Its burden holds it there," completes the first and gets repeated three times until the song fades away.

I did know what he meant. When we recorded that, I felt like we had moved beyond, far beyond, the mocking, not entirely serious, and certainly not grounded in reality, lyrics of most death metal. He held out the knife again, then pulled it away as I reached for it.

"You can't resist signing, in blood or otherwise, because you have already done so at the core of your being. Again, I do not know how, of all people, you laid claim to the ability to map the topography of that hidden landscape inhabited by the truest mystics, to record the sound of that truest secret whispered across the centuries from the dead to the living, but you have done so. Perhaps it is not you and I should be speaking now with the Spaniard instead, but that is neither here nor there. He and I will meet, I am sure, in due time. You think I want you to cut yourself, but you have already forgotten that I have first cut myself. You ask me what I am offering you, but overlook the fact that I have offered you my blood. Did Plutonic ever offer you that? Through my blood, I offer you my oath, and it is a simple one: Despondent Abyss will nurture you as an artist. You will belong to something greater than your previous label could offer. By joining forces with us, you should know that you, too, offer an oath. You swear to continue on the true calling of your soulside journey, you pledge to walk the path of shadows for eternity."

Although I was hooked on his words, I also knew it sounded ridiculous, this speech mired in metal cliché, in the same lyrical conventions he'd mocked, ridiculed, cursed to death death death in his letter. *Soulside Journey* is the name of the first Darkthrone album. There is no hidden landscape. The dead are just that, dead. Plus, blood or not, he wasn't offering me any of the trappings of music stardom, golden limousines or a diamond Rolex, the kind of baubles fit to ensnare some MC Faust proficient with an 808. He was offering me a chance to make another album, another forty minute exercise in lo-end belching that might appeal to a "select" audience of record hoarding miscreants spattered across the globe. That was it. There was nothing mystical or predestined about it, despite what he said, his talk of quests for destiny. Still, it appealed to some part of me, the dungeon-dwelling, D20 throwing child who, in some small way, believed in that sort of thing.

"You cannot resist this oath. Your core being, I see, has already immersed itself in spiritual blackness. As the poet Novalis says, 'Fate and temperament are two words for one and the same concept.' Besides, if you were to draw your card at this moment, spread the tarot, let's say, to guide you in your choice, you would see that you have no choice. You would draw the card of the traveler, I am certain. Look at you. You are regaled like a traveler, a pilgrim on a quest. And where does the word 'oath' come from, but 'ei,' 'to go through or towards'? And yet you already know the end point of your quest if you stay on the path set for you by your current label. It is a circle, a loser's lap around the fringes of Europe, and it ends where it starts, in your vapid homeland and you with nothing, not even a scar, to show for it. You must and will take the oath because you know that is your only escape, the only chance to feed the beast that spawned *In Circle of Ouroboros*. If you assent, you nurture your art. If you do not, its dried husk, a carcass called 'possibility,' will haunt you forever."

I think the specter of home is what made me do it, the haunting specter of failure. I picked up a purple toothpick from the now-empty cheese plate and jabbed it into my palm. A bead of blood welled up and I smeared it on a cardboard beer coaster.

"Okay, I'm with you. Consider this a contract."

He took the beer coaster and stuffed it in his jacket. He pulled out a CD and handed it to me.

"And now we begin our work. Take this and study it well. And remember," he flashed the horns, "don't break the oath."

Just then, the girls came in from the terrace, chattering like flittering birds. As they walked by our table, Nekrokor grabbed Thalia by the waist, dragged her to him, and slapped her ass.

"So, shall we go and see if your parents are home?" he asked.

He squeezed her thin thigh, his sharp fingernails leaving

tiny white crescents in her tan skin. His groping eroded her smile, but for some reason, she let him touch her. He pulled her onto his lap, and she kicked her legs up so she fell with all of her weight onto his crotch. Grete and I looked at each other awkwardly.

"I am going to see a movie now," she asked. "Would you like to come?"

"I think that sounds good. Thanks."

I stuffed the CD in my pocket, looking at it just long enough to make out the name "Astrampsychos," followed by a code, "DA 001," along the edge.

"I need to get my bike. I parked it nearby."

We left the bar and went to her bike. Grete pulled some keys out of her purse, a multicolored woven bag that looked like an oversized hacky sack, and unlocked it. Thalia and Nekrokor, leather jacket slung over one shoulder, his other arm around her waist, walked past us without saying a word. When they reached the corner, Thalia unwrapped herself from Nekrokor's grasp.

"Shall we go?" Grete asked. I nodded and we set off, the bike between us.

The movie, a Danish social realist downer, chronicled the inexorable decay of one family in a remote Greenland fishing village. There were English subtitles which seemed like all the combinations you could think of to restate Vizzini's excoriation of Andre the Giant in *The Princess Bride*: "And you ... unemployed ... in Greenland!" I folded and unfolded my arms, not sure what I was allowed to do, what I wanted to do, especially when expansive long shots of glaciated cliffs, set to mournful yet uplifting Arvo Pärt motets, flooded the theater in light, illuminating Grete's snow white thighs, snow white page boy, innocent face, and illuminating how close my hands were, or could be. Luckily, these moments of light were few and far between. Most of the scenes consisted of jerky hand-held shots in some grim cabin decorated in the disco era, then abandoned to the continual onslaught of many winters.

Why didn't I want to touch her? I mean, wasn't this a date of sorts, and me a traveling musician? Maybe it was the soundtrack, or the overall fatalistic mood of the film, but I couldn't work up the gusto. I kept imagining Natasha, still in Miami, probably not even aware of my world tour, on a date, the same kind of date, her and some dude, probably that dude from Abel's art happening, wedged together in the Cameo Theater off Lincoln Road while a more optimistic and whimsical movie, some magical realist central American fabula, recounted a similar lesson: "to forgive is to suffer."

• • •

At the end, everyone had died. The cabin still stood, but a devastating blizzard loomed.

"That's how all Scandinavian movies end," Grete said, straddling her bike. "With everyone dead."

We stood in front of the gothette townhouse, and I made a big show of writing down her phone number on the ticket stub and putting it in my wallet.

"Well, I hope that you call me before you leave Trondheim."

"Definitely," I said and leaned in for an awkward side hug interposed by a tangle of handlebars and brake cables.

I opened the door to the townhouse. Grete's bicycle hissed down the otherwise silent street, its turbine-powered light flickering in the never quite dark Trondheim summer night. I knew I'd never call her, a sentiment I felt strongest when, after the movie, she stopped at a pay phone to call her mom and explain where she'd been and when she'd get home. I don't know Norwegian, but the conversation took on a frantic and aggrieved tone after she said "American musician," a recognizable cognate.

The house was quiet, but I didn't feel reassured until I lay on the bath towel on the cold kitchen tile. I expected a hefty pink arm, a porcine thigh, to envelop me at any moment. Would Grete end up like these girls? I hoped not.

I tugged a scratchy wool blanket up to my neck and took the Astrampsychos CD out of my jacket, which I then zipped, slowly and soundlessly, to the top to hold in the heat otherwise pulled through the thin towel and into the unforgiving tiles. Norwegian summer nights might be bright, but that doesn't mean they're warm.

I slid the booklet out of the case and flipped through it. A two-page essay, printed in glacial blue ink on a black background, took up the center spread of the six-page booklet. Everything else, except for the band name, "Astrampsychos," and release code "DA 001" on the CD spine, was completely black. I recalled our conversation about Metallica. I held, I thought, the "true" black album. My eyes followed the small scrawly font snaking across the pages, but none of the undulations sparked any words I could recognize. It was too late, too dark to decode. All I could make out was the title: "On Life and Total Death." And a signature. The name of my erstwhile new employer, Nekrokor.

Juan came into the kitchen, naked except for his turban, which he'd fashioned into some kind of baldric/loin cloth combo.

"What's the story, champ?" he asked, pouring himself a glass of orange juice.

"I think we signed to a new label."

13. On Life and Total Death

I woke up with the booklet centered over my eyes, like a glossy paper sleep mask. Or death mask. The blue on black Nekrokor essay was no easier to read in the morning light. Imagine a CD gatefold crammed with all-caps Teutonic hieroglyphs:

> TOTAL DEATH IS A SYSTEMATIC PURSUIT OF ENDINGS, OF DEATH. WE HAVE CREATED THE AUDIAL ESSENCE OF EVIL, A TORTURE RITUAL IN PURSUIT OF DEMISE, NOTHINGNESS, ENDINGS. TO CREATE A SONG IS TO BRING ABOUT ITS END.

I slowly decoded it, holding the booklet in one hand while ambling around the kitchen in a search for coffee supplies. I found some Nescafe crystals and an electric tea kettle. By the time I sat down at the kitchen table with a steaming cup of coffee, I'd managed to read, and mostly understand, the first paragraph. If only it came with some multiple choice comprehension questions so I could quiz myself on its dual themes: a mystical pursuit of death and a commercial goal to sell albums to "fans" they openly despise.

Total death is a systematic pursuit of endings, of death. We have created the audial essence of evil, a torture ritual in pursuit of demise, nothingness, endings. To create a song is to bring about its end. You have removed the joy of discovery of that specific combination of notes to all people and forever. We pursue this wholehearted devotion to endings, to the death of musiks, as well in our spreading of the melancholy vision of Romantic poets like Heinrich Heine or Edvard Grieg. We use their materials to invert their transcendence, to show that they offer not transcendence, but a celebratory descendence into all those things considered hateful by Judeo Christian society. By employing their materials, we create them anew. By crafting our songs, we further limit the image of what is imaginable. We do this to precipitate the ultimate realm of featureless black, the trance-like fog of total death.

The stairway creaked as Juan and Delphine eased downstairs. They came into the kitchen, her thick arm curled around his neck like a water-logged life jacket.

"Where's Olienna?" I asked, putting the booklet on the table.

"She left earlier in the morning. Work. She said she was sorry she wouldn't be able to see us off at the station."

"I'm leaving today, too," Delphine said. "Back to Gent."

"Well, we'll see you soon, though," Juan said, massaging Delphine's arm.

"In a little over a week," he added, kissing her wrist.

"I don't think we're playing Gent," I interjected. The name didn't sound familiar. "We don't have any more Norway shows."

Juan and Delphine laughed.

"Gent's in Belgium, David. Hundreds of miles from here. It's where Delphine lives."

"I work for a Norwegian company with a factory there.

And I go to university. I grew up here."

Juan interjected, "I checked the schedule. We have a free day before our last show in Antwerp. We can stay there, with Delphine."

"It's very close to Antwerp, if you are concerned," Delphine said. "An hour by train."

Juan, unprompted, stepped into the kitchen, slid two slices of bread into the toaster, and retrieved a jar of purple jam from the refrigerator.

"Here, David. Let me make some breakfast before we head out."

I said that'd be fine—Juan had to be pretty keen on this girl if he stooped to this show of usefulness. Besides, I thought, I'm sure I can entertain myself while they spent a day humping.

As Juan spread jam—lingonberry, Delpine called it—on the toast, I told them about my meeting with Nekrokor. As soon as she heard the name "Nekrokor," she tried to change the subject, going on and on about the majesty of lingonberries, a specifically European delight. I opened up the booklet and showed the unreadable lettering to Juan, who said, "It's like a death metal Rosetta stone!" as Delphine launched into a tale of a childhood trip to pick fresh berries, she and her friends scouring the mountainside with fruit-laden wicker baskets.

"You've got to hear it, too. It's like a manifesto."

My finger traced down the page, "'Trance . . . like . . . fog . . . of total death.' Oh, I'm a bit past that. Here you go. . . ."

I took a sip of coffee, then started reading:

We are the true purveyors of death metal and thus strip that title from the bands crassly promoted with that vague genre designator to school children and idiots. If you are either of these, then be forewarned that you have made the wrong purchase. While we value your money, which we will use to build Satan's empire on earth, we do not recognize you. We give you total death.

"I like it!" Juan said, "Satan commands you to buy this album, sucker. This is the guy we need to work with!"

"Oh, it gets better." I skimmed ahead a bit. "I think he cracks on Valhalla in this next bit."

We are the true purveyors of death metal. What is it other bands convey through songs on environment, social injustice, and, worst of all, emotions? They create what should more accurately be termed 'life metal,' essentially cheerful music or, even more idiotically, hopeful music designed to encourage child listeners to fight for a better day.

"Do you know anything about this guy?" I asked Delphine. Trondheim's pretty small. I figured all the freaks must know each other.

"No. No, I do not know him." She put down her toast, her neck and cheeks flushed like ripe lingonberries. "But I have heard bad things."

"Like what?" Juan urged, but she wouldn't talk.

"Bad things like pulling a knife on me!" I cut in. "Sending me a death threat letter! I told you about that. Dude's looped, that's for sure. But he likes what we're doing. A bit of a philosopher, too. An educated madman. Listen to this . . ."

The true point of death metal is not to evoke an angry reaction. If you feel anger, the desire to engage in pointless rebellion, then you have listened incorrectly. The true point of death metal, the point at which it transforms, comes through the inward reaction it provokes. Ours then is the true path. Ours is the true path for we have fully renounced life in lyrical expression and musical arrangement. We have tuned down the pegs, enacting an essentially sephirotic transformation through our music. It is a spiritually black dimension we inhabit and that we evoke in all ways. Individually, we have found our lives guided by an ancient force, an evil entity, content to use our fleshly husks to protect and nurture its existence in this spiritual plane. In exchange for our service, really a form of the most complicit subservience, we do not seek to gain happiness or fulfillment. Instead, we seek only total death, and only to spread its festering grip.

Delphine sat, chewing. She glared at the purple jelly globs on her plate. She said, "I can understand why you may want to work with this Nekrokor, but you should be very careful."

• • •

After several increasingly unsatisfying shows at dismal factory towns of the Rhine valley, I began to regard Trondheim as the highpoint, and not just the starting point, of the Katabasis tour. It became clear, with each show, that what Nekrokor said about Plutonic was right. Sean hadn't sent posters to the clubs, the promoters were only dimly aware we were supposed to play, then didn't want to pay us—told me, after we played, that they'd been directed to mail the money to Plutonic headquarters in the States.

After a particularly ill-attended show in Kreutzfeldt, the club owner didn't pay us, then confiscated Juan's guitar and wouldn't let us leave until *we* paid *him*. For our electricity usage.

"This is not America," he'd said, "where you act like such things are free."

The crowds were no treat, either. Compared to German audiences, the Norwegians grooved like Solid Gold dancers. On each of our three German gigs, our so-called fans stood silent, staring at my fingers, and that's it. Some, arms crossed, tapped their fingers on their forearms as though they were air guitar stenographers transcribing every riff. And the other thing Nekrokor had said—that we merely shadowed

Metallica's succession of European tour dates—came back to me whenever our train pulled into some smoggy burg. As soon as the train doors accordioned open and we got our gear onto the platform, a mob of Metallica-shirted krauts hopped onboard, ready to ride the lightning right out of town.

In Prague, at least, someone waited on the platform to guide us. Not a fan, just some blue collar Czech making do in a postcommunist economic landscape by ferrying clueless newly arrived tourists to rooms in people's apartments.

"No rip off. Cheaper than a hotel," this guy, Jiří, told us as he stooped to lift my guitar case, a tiny gold cross hanging from his neck.

He guided us down a long mine shaft of an escalator and into the Metro. With its long row of crystal chandeliers gleaming above a burnt sienna marble floor, the platform looked more Cinderella's ballroom than grotty subway.

Pirate garbed or not, Juan shared the commonly-held view in south Florida that communism represented evil in its purest form. He used Jiří's cross as a way to segue into an entire litany of questions about the recently passed Soviet era.

"I see you wear a cross. Was it hard when the Communists restricted religion?"

Jiří's answers didn't give Juan what he wanted to hear. He said, "I did not need what this signifies, hope through suffering, until the Communists left."

Juan plied Jiří with more questions. "But things have improved, right? My parents escaped from Cuba. They told me what it was like."

"Things are very different now. Before, there was no worry. We had stability."

Juan reasked and rephrased his questions, like he thought Jiří just hadn't understood him correctly.

"But what I mean is . . . what about . . . what about freedom?"

Jiří set down the two guitar cases, the keyboard, and

Juan's heavy bag and dug a handful of coins out of his front pocket.

"Freedom?" He laughed, then shoved the coins into the Metro ticket machine. "What does that mean? The freedom to track down tourists day after day? The freedom to worry I will make enough to pay the rent and feed my children?"

He handed each of us a small yellow ticket.

"The only good thing is that we still have many protections. The government is not so stupid as to abandon the older generation. But I'm sure they will strip those away by the time I am old."

"But won't it be better for them? Your children?"

What Jiří said would be front page news in *The Miami Herald*: "Former Communist Alleges Communism Not All Bad." Then he'd be drawn and quartered by a mob. Him, or, at the very least, some piñata effigy.

"It will be better for them only because they will know no different."

He shouldered the bags, then hustled through the turnstile.

"The train we need is over this way."

That quieted Juan for awhile. I wondered if Jiří's life wasn't better than mine. When he mentioned protections, I thought of the time one of our assistant managers got sick, some weird skin ailment, and was out for a week. They fired her. Even as a full timer, I didn't have health insurance. I had no protections, and didn't expect any to come my way anytime soon.

Jiří guided us out of the Metro and onto a street tightly packed with gray concrete apartment towers. Flowerboxes speckled with yellow and pink blooms hung out of some of the windows. Spray painted tags marred the walls, and sometimes windows, of others. It looked like the apartments were filled with equal numbers of grandmas and gangsters. As he opened a rusted door leading in to a rusty stairwell, I hoped for grandmas.

On the way up, I asked Jiří for directions to the venue. He

had only the vaguest idea of where to find the club destined for our Katabic assault.

"People live here their whole lives, and still get lost," he said before giving us a map of Prague.

"No extra charge," he told us, "Not everyone would do this. Head back to the city center with the Metro. There's a Metro plan on the reverse."

Inside the apartment, a middle aged couple, he, bald, moustached, she, permed and in a floral print dress, sat on matching recliners and read matching newspapers as Jiří showed us the apartment—two beds, bathroom with hot water, six or seven locks that had to be undone in the correct order. The rooms had green wall paper covered in prints of blooming vines. Everything was shabby chic, except for the pictures hung in golden frames around the room—no oil paintings of puppies, or cornucopias, or still lifes of summer fruits. Each one had centerfolds of nekked ladies jazzercising in various combinations of head bands, leg warmers, and earmuffs. Jiří stood by the door, fingering his necklace. Juan peered at one of the pictures like it was some long lost Manet.

The lady in the recliner turned the newspaper page, and, with a slight nod, registered our presence. But none of the Czechs felt the need to explain the wall "art." Were these their daughters? Hourly workers, like me? I peeked over Juan's shoulder. No visible nametags, not even on a head band.

I ducked into the bathroom to piss. Before I shut the door, I said, "Hey Juan, can you tip the guy?"

It was no girlish tinkle. I unleashed a long yellow stream, sniffing the asparagus-y tones. Need to hydrate more. Hard to do on a continent without water fountains. I flushed, checked my chin stubble in the bathroom's gold framed mirror—should have had Juan keep the razor blades on his axe—then stepped back out into the living room.

Jiří still stood in the doorframe. Juan hadn't moved, either.

"For fuck's sake, Juan," I said as I pulled out my wallet and handed Jiří some money. "Thanks, man. Thanks for the map, too."

He muttered something under his breath and stuffed the folded bills in his shirt pocket. I felt embarrassed, like it was my fault Juan didn't know how to tip. Maybe this is how Gale felt all the time? I studied the map, pulled Juan away from the framed centerfold of a fur-bikini-clad redhead licking a banana, and headed down the grim musty steps into the city. On our way back to the Metro, a cold haze obscured the upper levels of the buildings. Flower boxes and graffiti tags faded into ethereal ghostliness. Cold rain dropped down as we shivered towards the station entrance. Juan pulled a pashmina fashioned out of unsold Katabasis t-shirts over his head.

I bought our tickets and guided us to the right platform. We stood under massive chandeliers on a reddish-brown marble platform waiting for the train.

"Look at those chandeliers. This is crazy. They built this as a subterranean palace for the proletariat."

If I knew him as well as Gale did, I'd recognize this fascination as the beginning of a new stage, soon to be complete with costume accessories, a cravat, maybe a monocle, something to evoke the enterprising gilded age industrialist who resisted the red tide. At the time, though, I thought he was talking about the present, about the real people who lived here now.

"Yeah, this'd be way better than sitting on some interstate. Still, it's like that guy was saying. Things are more open now, but also harder. I mean, he probably had a good job and now he's hanging out in the train station, working as a tourist valet. If it were me, I'd prefer the Communismo."

"No fucking way, David." Juan glared. "You don't know what that's like. My parents fought like hell to escape that. That's like an idiotomachy, where there's no room for anybody who's different at all. You know why they have chandeliers dotown here? It's because the common person living a common life is the ideal. That's what they want. They want to reward mediocrity."

"Ah no, dude. Think about it. You could just work your job, come home to your place, stick nudie pix on the wall. It's like . . . everyone's got the same stuff. Well, maybe your neighbor's got Miss November and you've got Miss June, but still."

To me, it was clear. That guy, Jiří, he was luckier than we'd ever be. If I lived here, I thought, it wouldn't be so bad to spend my life hustling copies of *Pride and Prejudice* for the Booksalot corporation. Or its Czech equivalent. I'd never fear the ground falling out under me, no money, never feel bad because I couldn't upgrade from a Pontiac Sunbird to a Ford Taurus. I could count on the train to whisk me from my crystal palace platform to my menial job for every day of my life, and then a guaranteed retirement. I'd never feel the need to leave that behind for the brief opportunity to hustle copies of *In Circle of Ouroboros* for the Plutonic corporation.

"There's not this expectation, this weight of having to prove yourself."

I'd been so taken by Prague's subway that I flouted one of the few social conventions of Miami conversation. Never suggest, in any way, to any Cuban, not even one dressed like Errol Flynn, that communism is not totally depraved, evil, and otherwise icky.

Juan turned his shoulder away, and pulled his little t-shirt hood forward so I could only see the tiniest tip of his nose. Natasha was the last person to snub me like this.

The train came. Its doors opened with a cheerful chime. Juan barged past an old lady trying to get off. She had on a pashmina too, but it was plum and not silk screened with Katabasis logos. When they collided, they looked like brawling Smurfs. I stepped out of the way to let her pass. She pushed a hand cart stuffed with carefully folded paper bags. I could see that she deserved more than a chandeliered commute. I smiled weakly and held the train door, although I don't know what good that would do if they came snapping shut—they didn't look safety equipped.

She gripped her cart, rattled it at me, and barked out something that sounded like "Doperdilla" in a low, husky voice. It sounded like the same thing that Jiří muttered after I tipped him. I don't think it meant "thank you."

I tried to sit next to Juan, but he moved away from me. Another move culled from Natasha's playbook. That's how it was in the months before the breakup. I was the target of her sullen dissatisfaction. I'd be too free—make a joke, call her "dude," spend too much time recounting Booksalot gossip—and she'd ignore me for awhile. A time out. What could I do? Cheat on him, too? How would that work? I thought of my Trondheim hangover. My shriveled penis in its latex pashmina. He wouldn't say what happened, just laugh and mime a violent barfing. It didn't help. I knew that part. Remembered it vividly. Delphine gave no details either. I asked her about it before we left. She just said, "There's a reason Olienna's not here to see you off. It's not because of her job."

I studied the map, traced our spelunk through the bowels of Prague. Rows of toothy, consonanty words—Pražskymhradem, Vrtbovská—spread across the images of towers, cathedrals, and ancient spires we'd soon find in the central city. I sounded them out, anything to contain my annoyance at Juan. Him mad at me? He couldn't even tip the train guy. He hadn't paid for a single thing so far on the tour. Now, he skulked at the far end of the Metro car. If I looked up at him, he'd turn his head. Another Natasha move. Maybe there was a reason I'd cheated on her? It had never occurred to me.

With one stop to go, the train rattled to a halt. The lights flickered out for a second, then back on. Juan still ignored me. None of the other passengers seemed fazed. A few exchanged knowing glances, pulled out magazines, newspapers, enormous volumes of literary classics.

I stared at the black emptiness framed by the train window for a few minutes. After a few minutes, Juan came over and sat next to me. My time out must have ended.

"See, this is exactly the kind of thing you'd endure daily, and worst of all, you'd be reliant on this. Your underground palace just a well-appointed waiting room."

Juan saw the stalled train as incontestable evidence that he was right, that I would, of course, recant my prior support of a fallen economic system.

He held out his hand, "Let me see that crazy Nekrokor thing."

I handed it over. The same thing would happen with Natasha, too. I'm always the apologetic one. The milquetoast. Maybe it was his bardic training, the way he'd resurrected the middle ages in the midst of art deco kitsch, but Juan had no problem breezing through line after line of the impenetrable codalith in the booklet:

> THE HARDCORE SCENESTERS, THE LIFE METALLERS ESPOUSING THEIR AFFIRMATIONAL LEFTIST POLITICS, CRITIQUE AS WELL OUR LIMITLESS PURSUIT OF GREED, OUR UNABASHED DESIRE FOR ALL TO HEAR, PURCHASE, AND MOST IMPORTANTLY, BE TRANSFORMED BY OUR RECORDS. THEY CLAIM TO OPPOSE A SINGLE-MINDED PROMOTION OF THEIR MESSAGE. THEY CLAIM TO EMBRACE THE VIRTUE OF NEVER SELLING OUT.
>
> WE LAUGH AT AND SPIT UPON SUCH A NARROW LACK OF SELF-INTEREST. WE HOPE TO SELL OUR RECORDS TO ALL COMERS. NOTHING WOULD PLEASE US MORE THAN INFANTS AND THE ELDERLY BATHED IN THE AURAL

> HOPELESSNESS WE SEEK TO TRANSMIT. THE ENTITY WE SERVE, WITH ITS LIMITLESS TALONS MANIPULATING US FROM THE CHAOTIC INFINITUDE OF SOME ADJACENT DIMENSION, SEEKS, FIRST AND FOREMOST, FOR THE PERVERSION OF ALL THAT IS HOLY.

which took me, reader, quite a bit of effort and keyboard pecking to render as:

The hardcore scenesters, the life metallers espousing their affirmational leftist politics, critique as well our limitless pursuit of greed, our unabashed desire for all to hear, purchase, and most importantly, be transformed by our records. They claim to oppose a single-minded promotion of their message. They claim to embrace the virtue of never selling out.

We laugh at and spit upon such a narrow lack of self-interest. We hope to sell our records to all comers. Nothing would please us more than infants and the elderly bathed in the aural hopelessness we seek to transmit. The entity we serve, with its limitless talons manipulating us from the chaotic infinitude of some adjacent dimension, seeks, first and foremost, for the perversion of all that is holy.

He agreed with most of it, too, laughing and muttering "that's right." While he read, I tried to pinpoint our exact position. I flipped between the Metro chart and the city map, figuring we had to be somewhere below the deepest crypt beneath St. Vitus cathedral, the skeletal toes of long dead bishops scraping the roof of the train.

Juan turned to me. "Crazy or not, I like this guy."

"You sure? You don't think he'll stab us?"

"No man. I'm sure that's part of his costume. His act." He held the booklet up. "You know, this stuff may sound scary—aural hopelessness and all that—but it's not like our music—your music—is much different. Gale started to get worried for me when I met you. The mix tape. That Valhalla album. Satanic Dominions. 'No resurrection, undead rises again.' That's some titillating stuff, too. She grew up with religious parents. Cuban Catholics. They don't mess around with religion. My parents are the same. That's one of the first things the Communists took. They give you a fancy subway, but take your spirit."

"This guy's serious, though."

A message came on over the train's loudspeaker. None of the locals budged.

"Good! That's what we need. A serious salesman. And a good one, I bet. He wants to sell records. And to do that, he's selling an image. That's what people want. A piece of that image, something beyond the tedium of most people's lives. Seriously? You meeting that guy is a huge success. Based on this thing alone," he thumped the booklet, "he's a hundred times better than these jokers you've been dealing with. Those guys don't care about us. It's like he told you. They sent us here to fall apart, to go back home feeling like we lost."

"Yeah. We have, haven't we?"

The train lurched, then paused, like a recalcitrant hairball facing down a plunger.

"No, David. You don't get it, man. You have to be strong, not let people push you around."

Was he being ironic?

"This is the start. And you know, I've been thinking about something since we got ripped off in Kreutzfeldt. That shit about sending the money back to those hillbillies. They're getting paid. What happens if we just don't show up?"

"Mmm." I hadn't thought about that. Phil would never have suggested it.

"They'll lose money. Granted, not much, based on the crowds we've had, but something. They'll lose something."

The train rattled its way down the thirty feet of track between us and our stop. By the time the train doors opened, Juan had me persuaded.

Prague was our first missed gig, but it wouldn't be the last.

14. To Winds ov Demise

The train slowed. A flat landscape of orderly green fields and compact red roofed houses gave way to the gray and brown tones of all cities. A lighted sign at the front of the car flashed a message, "Wij komen aan in Gent St. Pieters." Passengers around us put away books and magazines, the tinny rattle of Discman techno the only sound as they formed a somber line in the aisle.

Juan stood up and swayed as the train came to a stop.

"This is it. We're here," he said.

We stumbled off the train as the other passengers quietly breezed past us and down a staircase.

Juan looked around, half expecting, I thought, to see Delphine there with a welcome banner and a dozen roses.

"Today's the 21st, right?"

I hoisted my backpack and followed the crowd down the staircase, a guitar case in one hand, a keyboard in the other. A light drizzle fell from a low gray sky as we stepped out of the train station. A brown, smoke-shrouded window fronted a railway cafe. Inside, waitresses serving sandwiches and crisps appeared as brown and hazy as characters in some century-old daguerreotype.

We passed a vast sea of bikes, of wheels, chains, gears in various stages of rusting decay. The occasional taxi-yellow bike punctuated the scene, like a dandelion in a yard of dead grass. I wondered how anyone could find their bike once they'd parked it.

A large group headed past the bikes and up a wide avenue towards what could only be the center of the city.

Juan stopped, transfixed.

"Where is she? We're meeting somewhere at three."

It wasn't quite noon. Typical Juan, expecting Delphine to stalk the station like a trainspotter.

"Where are we supposed to meet her?" I asked, trying to control my annoyance.

Juan smiled, then dug his hand into his satchel.

"Wait . . . I just remembered. She wrote it down. I have it in here."

He pulled out his plane ticket, stuffed it back in, then produced a beer coaster and showed it to me. In orderly, girlish cursive, it read "St. Baafs cathedral, 3 PM, June 21."

Seeing the plane ticket threw me from annoyance into panic. Who cared if we found Delphine or not? In three days, we'd be in Amsterdam, boarding a direct flight from Schiphol, the Netherlands to Shithole, Florida. There was no mystery there. I knew exactly what horrors awaited me once the attendant took my boarding pass. I'd be dropped from Plutonic which, despite what Nekrokor had said, I still regarded as the better record label. I'd have to beg for my job. That would be the end of my rock and roll fantasy.

We stopped at a city map set up in a small park directly across from the entrance to the station. There was some kind of stonehengish rock circle around a door-sized map, like the kind you'd find in a mall.

"Let's check out that map. Did she give you any directions?"

"No. She just said it's in the city center."

I traced out potential routes, a pile of luggage and instruments at my feet. As the crowd from the station cleared out, I started to feel self-conscious and exposed. Juan, in a top hat and Katabasis shirt covered by a paisley vest, didn't exactly help us to blend in. A group of Eurogangsters, dressed head to toe in baby blue Sergio Tacchini gear, sat on some nearby benches. Even without Juan, you can't really blend in when you're wearing a massive hiking backpack and carrying instrument cases. You feel like you're carrying a sign that says, "Rob me!"

His antics didn't help. He gamboled around the rocks, leaping from stone to stone like a Cirque de Soleil tumbler. I felt like "Juan Bon Joker" wasn't such a bad name after all. What good would he be if these kids tried us, made a move, exploited our obvious cluelessness?

Juan balanced on one leg and pointed at a tram.

"David—that one says 'Saint Baafs'!"

He dug his hand into his pocket, unleashing a shower of subway tickets, receipts, and coins. The kids across the way watched carefully as his kroners, marks, and crowns rolled across the ground. They watched as my money, my kroners, my marks, my crowns, lay scattered in the dirt.

In Miami, he'd never pay me back. I thought of my bank balance bottoming out over two weeks, plummeting with each ATM receipt. If I graphed it, you'd see a sheer cliff. A sinkhole of emptiness where once there was money.

Over a year of working at Booksalot, I'd somehow managed to save something like $6,000. It wasn't so hard to do. Drink the free coffee. Buy the cheap beer. In just two weeks, I'd spent nearly half of that. A stack of unsold Katabasis CDs sat at the bottom of my pack. We hadn't even sold twenty.

I did not want to be jammed in a crowded tram with Juan on display, and me the only one expected to know the way. I did not want to spend any more time at the nearly deserted train station.

"Come on, man. Let's get moving."

I hoisted my backpack, grabbed a music case in each hand, and set off towards a crosswalk.

"Wait, David!"

"It looks like we just follow that road to the center of the city. We can ask someone for directions there."

Juan bumbled behind me, stuffing coins into his pocket, his leather satchel, even tucking one or two into the brim of his top hat. Pedestrians glared as they sidestepped this costumed buffoon, this role playing leech. The gangstery kids rocked with laughter. One stood on the rocks by the map, imitating Juan. The good thing about going home, I thought, is that I wouldn't be his caretaker anymore. I felt like a Mickey Mouse docent, a cartoon animal trainer. I felt like the guy who guides the guy in the costume, keeps kids from headbutting his groin.

Maybe, I thought, that's what I could do when I get back? I could get a job at Disney. I'd get to wear a nametag.

• • •

After ten minutes or so, we crossed a six lane road separated by a wide tree lined median. Then, we followed the street through a residential neighborhood of apartment blocks punctuated by the occasional pub. The regular rhythm of Juan's wheeled duffel bag bumping down the sidewalk broke the silence. I suppose it was the middle of a work day, but the city felt a little too quiet.

Ahead, the road continued without any break or change. As we crossed the first intersection we'd seen in some time, I saw some landmark, a theater or a museum, its front marked with the word "Vooruit" spelled out in tiles, at the crest of a cobblestoned hill.

"Let's turn here. Maybe we can ask for directions up there?"

As we walked up the hill, the duffel bag bucking against the cobblestones like an enraged mule, we started to pass a series of window displays: sleek, snap together office furniture; paper white nude mannequins with new wave wigs; photos of houses and condos topped with Dutch phrases like Te Koop and Te Huur. We had to be getting closer to the city center.

We passed a window filled with CDs, posters, a rainbow of

vinyl hanging from fishing line.

"A music store. Let's look there instead."

As I walked past, I noticed a familiar scrawl on a poster advertising a new album called *Embalmed Entrails*. In Human Form. I knew them. They were from Tampa. Their demos got reviewed in the same zines as ours. Those guys might have seen us play, even. I corrected myself. Might have seen John and Phil and Jake and I play. They'd done well for themselves. The poster had the Plutonic Records seal of approval. It also had the Dan Seagrave cover art we'd turned down. I'd turned down. Because it didn't "match," according to Juan, our album's arcane "concept." On the poster, the dual stars of a far off universe cast a purple and orange sunset on some living malevolent city. This, you could tell, was a real death metal album, all blast beats and complex riffs. A hellish chasm of sound.

Just seeing the album made me angrier, more anxious. Maybe I could work as their roadie if, you know, the Disney thing didn't pan out? Juan hadn't noticed. Instead, he cooed, pointing at a picture of the Chieftains, a bunch of beardy dudes standing in a fishing boat.

"Ooh. Maybe I can get something there for Delphine."

I turned the corner and ducked into the store, half hoping Juan would just saunter past.

• • •

My growing annoyance with Juan, my fear of returning, fell away as I opened the door to this shop, the Record Huis. I stepped off cobblestones probably hammered into place by a dyspeptic plague victim and into a space marked by the iconology of modern pop music. No matter the circumstances, a good record shop can heal all wounds.

A multicolored explosion of stickers wallpapered the interior. A gauzy pop song—Mazzy Star, I thought—jangled through the store. On the wall by the cash register, I could make out the Beastie Boys kickin' it curbside in flannel and gazelles, the SweeTart pastels of a Stereolab poster, the dried plum bug squashed across the drab olive background of a Dinosaur Jr. sticker. The store had separate sections for each genre. The employees had decorated the sides of the aisles with favorite picks, new artists, and lists of upcoming albums for every kind of music imaginable. To my right, ballerinas tip toed across a glimmering blue lake while Yo Yo Ma wrapped his arm around a muppet. Farther back on that side, medievalish middle-aged minstrels beamed at the camera, hoisting mandolins and lutes. The pop section took up much of the rest of the store. In the back left corner, the dense collage of promotional materials abutted a sticker-free area painted a light-sucking matte black. A single silver pentagram hung from the ceiling like some kind of anti-disco ball.

I dropped my bags off with Juan, who had, unfortunately, found his way into the store and started rifling through the racks. Stepping into the metal section was like stepping into a different store. Mazzy Star's sultry chanteuse still sang of love and longing, but it sounded like thick gray felt encased the speakers. The stripped down display stripped the notes from the air. The barren sparseness extended to the inventory, too. I stood between two aisles. On the left, you could buy music by maybe ten bands. They stocked huge quantities of a few key albums: Bathory's *Blood Fire Death*, Celtic Frost's *To Mega Therion*, Destruction's *Eternal Devastation*, and Venom's *At War With Satan*. I looked for the In Human Form album, but couldn't find it.

The second aisle testified to the artistic output of some band I'd never heard of, something called "Desekration." There were flyers, t-shirts, even beer-opening key chains emblazoned with the name of this one band. The logo came courtesy of Destruction. The "k" looked like a "t" with its left cross removed, then taped diagonally below the right cross. The other "t" was, naturally, inverted. You could see that these guys had forged an "a" from a monstrous melding of a "u" and "c." Who knows? It could have been "Desekrotion."

Instead of:

you had this:

Or rather, one guy was the graphic designer. The singer, guitarist, and drummer, too. An 8x10 photo, black and white, perfectly centered and evenly taped, showed the mastermind of this project. He wore corpsepaint, by which I mean his face was plastered with white make up, think cold cream or Coppertone, except for his eyes and mouth, which were smeared with black. You could say he looked like someone from KISS but, as I'd learn, the purpose and practice of corpsepaint is about as far from "Detroit Rock City" as you can get.

He had on a studded leather jacket. Bullet belts and barbed wire looped around his body. The branches of a dead tree, spindly as spider legs, filled the background. Flecks of snow speckled the photo. In his right hand, he brandished a stick with long roofing nails driven through it at impossible angles. The stick didn't look like a branch so much as the handle of a plunger modified into a weapon, a plumbing tool for particularly calcific caca. You couldn't see the end of the DIY mace. Was there a working broom or mop sitting in the snow somewhere beyond the photo frame? And where was his other hand? His left arm stretched towards and above the lens, like he was holding the camera. It was a self-portrait of this guy, on some cold Belgian night, standing in the snow, holding a modified broom, and glowering at his Instamatic.

Below the photo, there were stacks and stacks of Desekration's musical output, a single 7-inch called "To Winds ov Demise." On the cover, a simple black and white photo, the tendrils of a dead tree's branches stretched from the center to each edge of the sleeve. It looked like the photographer had lain on the ground with his feet against the trunk, the uneven flash illuminating some of the branches but not quite getting others, which disappeared into the night. The serpentine branches intertwined with a centered "Desekration." Below, the words "To Winds ov Demise" wound across the cover.

A tattered, handwritten flyer hung next to the photo, the bottom of the page fringed with the number to the official Desekration hotline:

DESEKRATION-COMPLETE BLASPHEMATION OF JERUSALEMS TRIBES

DESEKRATION-FULFILLMENT OF SATAN DIVINE PROPHECY

DESEKRATION-FIRST STRIKES OF DIABOLICRUSADE

DESEKRATION-SEEKS DRUMMER, GUITARS, AND VOCAL

As I read the flyer, wondering why "blasphemation" and

"diabolicrusade" *weren't* actual words, a huge mountain of a guy came up to me and started speaking Dutch. It sounded kind of like English, but mellifluous and mumbly all at once, like a clarinet, or the honks of a territorial goose.

I stared blankly. He switched to English.

"I see you guys bring instruments. You here to audition?"

Compared to his get up in the Desekration poster, this guy was a bit dressed down for work, but not by much. Three or four bulletbelts cris-crossed his paunchy belly. A massive yellow bush of hair added at least a few inches to his height. He towered over me, regarding me through bulbous, almost gouty, eyes set deep under a thick ledge of an eyebrow. Somewhere along the line, he counted *Homo neandertalis* as a direct descendent.

No corpsepaint. Instead, a nametag. J. Svart.

"Uh?" Was I here to audition? I looked over at Juan, who flipped through a thick stack of potential love tokens. He was holding at least $100 worth of merchandise. Maybe I was. It looked like Juan would be occupied for the next day or so. At the very least, maybe I could sell this Svart guy a Katabasis CD, or trade one for "To Winds ov Demise," a souvenir of my Eurotour.

"Yeah, I think so. I play guitar. What exactly are you looking for?"

He explained his vision, something stripped down and raw. Something that he repeatedly called "cold" or "cult," he used the words interchangeably.

"This one," he held up the 7-inch, "is the cornerstone. But true is, it is repetitive and poor produced. Next one, Desekration's *Infernö*, that will be the essence of cult."

I told him about our tour, about Katabasis and Valhalla. I had job experience. He'd heard of Katabasis, he'd said, which seemed strange. Very few people have heard of Katabasis. Whenever I said the phrase "death metal" though, he furrowed his brow. I mentioned the In Human Form album I saw in the display.

He smirked, unimpressed.

"That band is not in the metal section. You can find them in 'pop.' You may not be meant to join Desekration. This is not a death metal band. Every album, always the same. Same cover art, same studio, same producer. Same sound. If you audition, you will not make that sound. I want the sound of cult, of ice, of winter."

I thought I'd take a different tack, make sure I'd even have the honor of auditioning. I told him about Katabasis, how we wrote the songs, recorded the album. I made it sound like we'd done all these things to deliberately de-deathmetal-ify the music. Then, once the slab-like brow defurrowed, I tried to regain control of the conversation, ask him the questions. I asked him where we'd go to play.

"The community center has a studio. It is very cheap and they have drum kit. I practice and record there. They put it in an old Begijnhof—it is like a nunnery, enclosed by walls. In our history, here women had freedom. When I record, I imagine all the old nuns having fun."

When I asked him if anyone had bought "To Winds ov Demise," it began to dawn on me that maybe I did want to audition.

"How many copies of, uh, 'To Winds ov Demise' have you sold?"

"Well, at first not so many. Lately, though, many more. People now feel the strike of diabolicrusade. I have just sold 500 in the states, to a mail order catalog. You may know it— Plutonic Records. This is the second shipment in two months. The label guys say even Americans tire of the death metal they created."

He'd sold more of that self-produced Xeroxed thing than Katabasis. In the states alone. Through my record label.

"Here. This is what I aspire to."

He handed me a CD.

"Astrampsychos. *The Intrapsychic Secret*. It just came out. Like their first, it is cult."

Astrampsychos. I remembered my recent "contract negotiations."

"Isn't some guy called Nekrokor in that group?"

"Dat klopt. He plays guitar. He is the best."

He pointed to a picture of Nekrokor, in corpsepaint, shirtless, arms crossed, the same knife he'd pulled on me clenched in his fist. The other band members were in similar poses. One, Nordikron, wielded a long, recently unearthed root like a whip, its hydra head lashes bristling with dirt clogged rhizomes. Below the song titles, there was a list of upcoming Despondent Abyss releases: another Astrampsychos album called *Yersina Pestiis*, something called *Secretum Diabolis* by Kontakion, and below that, *The Gate of Horn* by Katabasis. I reread it several times. It said Katabasis, us, and not some other band, Katobasis or Kutubasik.

What the hell, I thought. It said Katabasis, meaning me. Juan stood at a listening station, headphones on, a huge stack of CDs on the counter. If I cut him off my payroll, I could last for a few months longer. Fuck the return ticket.

"Yeah, I'm definitely here to audition" I reached out and passed the CD back to this guy, J. Svart. "I think you're going to be interested in what I can bring to the table."

15. Masher of Puppets

I didn't tell Juan about our Nekrokor-planned forthcoming release, though I could have easily showed it to him. I had a Despondent Abyss flyer in the Desekration swag bag Svart pushed on me once he realized he was talking to a genuine Despondent Abyss artist, a harbinger of all that is kvlt. It was stuffed with stickers, a sew-on patch, and a complimentary copy of "To Winds ov Demise" with Svart's telephone number Sharpied across the top.

"Listen to this and think it over. Get in touch only if you are serious. I am here all day, when the shop opens," he said as he gave it to me.

Besides, Juan didn't ask. Instead, he pestered me to buy something from the massive stack of world music he balanced in his palm.

"It's just polite to bring a gift when you're staying with a guest."

"Here—you can give her these." I crammed a couple of Desekration stickers in his outstretched hand and stepped out of the store.

He hurried to catch up to me.

"We should come to the main square if we follow this road. I asked about it while you were talking to that guy. We're going to something called St. Baafsplein. It's a big meeting spot in front of the cathedral."

We walked along a busy shopping street, passing stores

for women's footwear, crowded pubs, and at least three shops with columns of slowly twirling kabob logs in their front windows. After a few blocks, the city opened up to us. We entered its center, three interconnected squares filled with life. A massive spire scraped the sky above each square. A round golden dragon hovered at the top of the middle tower. It looked like a plump shoarma stick pinioned to the steeple. A tram slid by on gleaming tracks. At the far edge of the city center, a horsedrawn buggy clopped across a gently arching bridge. Crowds of people sat outside at the cafes fronting each square. Not even Disney, I thought, could have imagineered a more perfect space.

Delphine stood on a midstreet median and waited as the tram snaked past. She was there, looking like a loving gnome's wife in a cobblestone-length lavender gown, her hair twined in pigtails. Reins for a lusty cattle drive. Beaming, she stepped off the curb across the street. In a dramatic flourish, Juan pulled his top hat off his head, reached inside, and produced a hand carved wooden puppet of a blue robed wizard, its cotton ball Gandalf locks topped with a pointed star-strewn hat.

I recognized it from one of the many puppet-laden street vendor carts we'd passed before and after the sumptuous goulash and pilsner meals I'd paid for in Prague. I hadn't seen him buy it, though. He did his souvenir shopping on the sly. Granted, Czech prices amounted to about $5 for a huge meal complete with drinks, but he never, not once, made a single move to empty his little coin pouch for me.

I had to restrain myself. The urge to punch him in the dead center of the stupid Ouroboros tattooed to his hairless birdchest churned my innards like a turbo powered blender. Right then, I hated him. Hated myself for everything I'd given him. Listening to his stupid ideas. Skipping the last few shows—quite possibly, the last shows I'd ever play—so he could traipse about Europe on my dime. Hated his self-absorbed monologues. His self-fellating snake.

I grabbed him by the shoulder, twisted him like a little

puppet.

"I paid for this tour, you cheap bastard. That doll. Whatever else you've got tucked away in your stupid fucking costumes. Me. Every train. Every meal. When I go back, I'll work five years to get back on my feet."

His smile disappeared. He said nothing, just glanced down his nose at me, his hat in one hand, the puppet in the other. He looked like Machiavelli machinating a plot to deliver a filigreed dagger to my gullet. I'd pissed him off, I could tell, because I'd been in this situation with him before. He was clearly in the wrong, but he looked at me like I'd violated some "point d'honneur." I could even imagine him thinking that phrase as he glared at me, his slightly downturned lips as blue gray as a cold mackerel in the seafood case.

He set the hat on the ground and hugged the wizard to his chest.

"Well, perhaps you should have been more responsible with your money."

Then, he turned his back to me, reached into his hat again, and pulled out another puppet—this time, a green dragon. He held them above his head and waved them at Delphine like a hyper kindergartner at show and tell.

I snapped.

I grabbed the dragon, and tossed it high above the Gent street scene. It landed with a plonk in front of the tram, which steamrolled it into a crumpled twig heap.

"Ha! Go buy another one! With your own money!"

I spun on my heel and stomped off, laden with bags, my guitar case hitting my knee with every step.

As I rounded the corner, disappearing into the jumble of twisting, narrow streets, I heard Delphine ask Juan, "What's the matter with him?"

• • •

I quickly lost myself in the mass of interconnected streets— alleys, really—winding between the low slung buildings radiating off of St. Baafsplein. My puppet mashing rage faded into a pleasant recognition of my roving solitude. I wandered alone, in silence, and just ten minutes earlier, I'd silently endured Juan going on about the city as a modern version of the Minotaur's labyrinth, which, he noted, was a monster sacred to the Triple Goddess, and its maze-like prison just another iteration of the omnipresent Ouroboros.

I wandered alone, with his incessant nattering behind me. And at my own pace, too. I didn't have to slow down every ten steps so Juan could catch up. Listen to him bitch about the non-ergonomic straps of his crappy little satchel. Accede to his endless requests or comments. Examine every touristical trinket produced from the Arctic Circle to the Eastern Bloc.

At first, I felt the teensiest twinge of guilt for ruining Juan's puppet. No need for histrionics or aggression. Like John and Phil's stepdad. Better to be cold and steely. Sinister. The left hand path. Left. I could have just left. I could have left in Prague, even, after he gave me the silent treatment. Or any other time when he jabbered over anything I had to say. Mooched my cash. Drank my drink.

My grievances quickly overshadowed any guilt—it shrank and faded away entirely as I moved through the streets. You know what else is sacred to the Triple Goddess? A cold beer. The treasure at the heart of the labyrinth. And I don't have to buy you another one again, bardic asshole, I thought, as I picked up the pace.

Let Delphine take care of him. Good luck. Hope your refrigerator's fully stocked.

I found myself nearing the city square again, even though I'd tried to move in the general direction of the train station. This time, the streets disgorged me by a bridge next to the smallest of the three towers. I didn't want to run into Juan and Delphine who, I felt, could be anywhere in this central and relatively exposed part of the city. Instead, I turned left and crossed the bridge. It arced over a canal flanked by sidewalk cafes packed with people who had never heard of

Death Metal Epic I: The Inverted Katabasis

Katabasis, the Ouroboros, the eternal quest for the Triple Goddess. They drank, talked, and seemed none the worse for their ignorance of mythic esoterism. Umbrellas emblazoned with ads for beers I'd never heard of—Hoegaarden, Leffe, Gulden Draak—topped each cafe table.

What would I do? I contemplated stopping somewhere for one of these beers. I couldn't put on our last show, the following day in Antwerp, by myself. Besides, would anyone be there to notice? My absence may inconvenience a few disconsolate Antwerper doomsters and their gothy consorts, but I figured they were probably used to disappointment.

Of course, no amount of stylized doom metal ennui could match the utter anguish, the total bummer, I'd feel in just a few days when my plane descended into Miami International.

My temporary escape from Hell thwarted.

And what then?

The only musicians I still knew—Abel and his hipster contingent—would never let me join one of their bands. And I surely couldn't conscript them, force them to play in my so-called band. Not even if I told them I had a contract. Signed in blood. They'd just laugh.

And even if I could, what would that sound like? My Despondent Abyss debut, *The Gate of Horn*, a carefully crafted batch of jaunty, postpunk, postteen love songs? *The Gate of Horny*? Nekrokor would ritually curse me again, no doubt. And who could blame him? I'd curse myself if I played such lame music.

I found a bar across the canal and well away from St. Baafsplein. I walked in, read the beer menu, and went with the Gulden Draak—named after the golden dragon at the top of the Belfort Tower.

Out of habit, I ordered two. Unconsciously, I turned to hand the second one to a bard who wasn't there.

Alone. With two beers. In a beautiful city. I could get used to this, I thought, as I carried both beers back to my table.

I could get used to this if I didn't go back. If I stayed. If I conscripted a true warrior of the diabolicrusade.

143

• • •

An aggressive snorer in the bottom bunk at the youth hostel prompted a rare, for me, bout of early birdism. As soon as I woke up, I headed from the hostel to that cafe, the Vooruit, across the street from Svart's record store, and waited for it to open. The Vooruit is more cafeteria than cafe. Inside, techno lite bumped gently as the morning crowd downed fruity pastries. I staked out a window seat and watched the city spring to life around me. Most of the city, that is. The record shop was a late sleeper. Its doors and windows stayed shuttered well into my third cup of tepid Belgian coffee. Coffee quality, I concluded, was the one, and maybe only, area where Miami holds the upper hand.

"Vooruit," the barista told me on one of my refill runs, means "progress." Apparently, it used to be some socialist meeting spot. Don't tell Juan. Vooruit—the first Dutch word I learned. I hope it's a sign. Some malevolent deity has pitied me and sought to maintain me as its servant. As I waited, I scrawled a budget, a list of goals, on a napkin.

The first figure on the napkin was the date and time of my return flight: July 24. 6:30 AM. As if convinced the date would magically transform, panicked that I'd already missed the flight, I also took out my return ticket and checked it repeatedly. While I had little trouble persuading myself to skip a flight that left out of Amsterdam in a mere 48 hours, the figure below the time, the price, kept me from committing to the plan. Stay. As long as possible.

I'd paid nearly $700 for the ticket. Tiny script on the front of the ticket read: "Tickets are nonrefundable and must be used on date of travel." I hate wasting money. I couldn't get past the fact that I'd waste a lot of money by not taking the return trip. I would waste the money I'd already spent.

I wrote the other important figure below that on the napkin. The balance listed on my most recent ATM receipt. A surprising $2,600. And the key hope for optimism. With Juan off my payroll, I could make this last awhile. I just wasn't sure if it was long enough to justify flushing $700 down the toilet. Was it worse to waste my life by going back home, or my money by staying here?

I figured I could scrape by for the rest of the summer, maybe even until Christmas, if I economized effectively. They must sell Top Ramen in Belgium, I thought. With some severe austerity measures in place and, more importantly, without Juan, I could possibly stick around in Gent for an entire year. Play in Desekration. See if Nekrokor is really serious about my music.

The only problem I could see was that my future fortunes depended on other people. Natasha. Juan. Phil. John. That hadn't worked for me yet. Why did I think things would be different with a blimpish Belgian and a knife-wielding Satanist?

Across the street, I detected movement: the metal security shutters fronting the record shop rattled up. Time for business. A thin, short haired indie rocker in peg pants and a striped t-shirt disappeared inside the record store. Minutes later, the front windows came to life as coiling strands of white Christmas lights illuminated sparkly LP covers.

I got another cup of coffee and continued my stakeout. By the time I reached the powdery dregs, Svart puffed up the hilly street leading from the train station. He pedaled a rickety black and rust colored bike, a stack of LPs clenched under one arm. Sweat plastered his black t-shirt to his skin. I hurried outside and met him as he caught his breath, his hands on his knees. He looked at me with wild eyes through his yellow pillow of hair, but didn't say anything.

At first, I thought he didn't remember me. Or he'd decided I wasn't serious enough, wasn't sufficiently cult. Maybe he could tell—could somehow sense I hadn't even listened to his record? He could sense that its tones had not blasphemated my being.

Was this the right move?

He still didn't say anything. I nearly walked away, to the

train station, the airport, and, in a best case scenario, the unavoidable descent into Booksalot wage slavery. Then, the number, my bank balance, popped into my head once more. It spurred me into action.

"Hey, I'm David. We talked yesterday. I'm serious about this. I listened to it. 'To Winds ov Demise'. It's fantastic," I lied. "I want in—sign me up for Desekration's *Infernö*!"

Continued in

THE GOAT SONG SACRIFICE

The Second Book
of the

Death Metal Epic

Acknowledgements:

Thanks to the following people, in no particular order, for their help at various stages of this project: Jeff Vrabel, James Ortega, Jason Snart, Eric Sanders, Andersen Prunty, Matthew Revert, D. Harlan Wilson, Lee Templeton, Paul Zimmerman, Branden Linnell, Digby Pearson, Pierre Bittner, the guys in Destruction, Eric Greif, Dan Seagrave, and Jurgen Vercruysse. Above all, thanks to my family for their love and support.

Quoted lyrics cited from Death's "Symbolic" (Mutilation Music/ Universal Music (BMI)), Moonspell's "An Erotic Alchemy" (Century Media records), Deicide's "Dead by Dawn" (Roadrunner records), and Cathedral's "A Funeral Request (Ethereal Architect)" (Earache records).

The Destruction logo appears courtesy of Nuclear Blast records.

I'm calling this series an epic, but really it's an extended work of devotion (or, rather, devotation) to the music I've listened to for so long. So, in true, death metal liner note fashion, I raise my chalice to the following for inspiration and musical accompaniment while writing: Nile, Obscura, King Diamond, Om, Blind Guardian, Mournful Congregation, Fenriz (in his guise as DJ), Behemoth, Ahab, Summoning, and, of course, every band mentioned in the book.

Dean Swinford likes all kinds of music—death metal, black metal, and doom metal. Everything but nu metal. He lives in North Carolina. This is his first novel.

CPSIA information can be obtained
at www.ICGtesting.com
Printed in the USA
LVHW041927030820
662267LV00009B/1729